STAR WARS

THE CLONE WARS

Adapted by Tracey West

Based on the
Star Wars:

Puffin Book

D1392347

PUFFIN BOOKS

Published by the Penguin Group
Penguin Books Ltd, 80 Strand, London WC2R ORL, England
Penguin Group (USA) Inc., 375 Hudson Street, New York, New York 10014, USA
Penguin Group (Canada), 90 Eglinton Avenue East, Suite 700, Toronto, Ontario, Canada M4P 2Y3
(a division of Pearson Penguin Canada Inc.)
Penguin Ireland, 25 St Stephen's Green, Dublin 2, Ireland (a division of Penguin Books Ltd)
Penguin Group (Australia), 250 Camberwell Road, Camberwell, Victoria 3124, Australia
(a division of Pearson Australia Group Pty Ltd)
Penguin Books India Pvt Ltd, 11 Community Centre, Panchsheel Park, New Delhi – 110 017, India
Penguin Group (NZ), 67 Apollo Drive, Rosedale, North Shore 0632, New Zealand
(a division of Pearson New Zealand Ltd)
Penguin Books (South Africa) (Pty) Ltd, 24 Sturdee Avenue, Rosebank, Johannesburg 2196,
South Africa

Penguin Books Ltd, Registered Offices: 80 Strand, London WC2R ORL, England

puffinbooks.com

First published in the USA in Grosset & Dunlap, an imprint of Penguin Group (USA) Inc., 2008
Published in Great Britain in Puffin Books 2008

1

Set in Linotype Sabon
Made and printed in England by Clays Ltd, St Ives plc

British Library Cataloguing in Publication Data
A CIP catalogue record for this book is available from the British Library

ISBN: 978-0-141-32509-5

www.greenpenguin.co.uk

Penguin Books is committed to a sustainable future
for our business, our readers and our planet.
The book in your hands is made from paper
certified by the Forest Stewardship Council.

PROLOGUE

Steady streams of spacecraft crowded the airspace above planet Coruscant. For years the planet had been the centre of government for the Galactic Republic, the democratic union that kept order throughout the galaxy.

Now the Republic was under attack. Count Dooku and his Separatist Alliance were causing chaos by invading planets along key trade routes. Chancellor Palpatine, the leader of the Galactic Senate, had committed thousands of clone troopers to defend those planets. These genetically engineered clone soldiers were superior to the Separatist droid armies in many ways. However, without strong leadership, they were no match against Dooku's massive assault.

Enter the Jedi. This peaceful order of galactic

guardians had taken to the battlefields during this conflict, becoming generals in command of the army of clone soldiers.

While battles raged across the galaxy, the citizens of Coruscant felt safe on the well-defended planet. Coruscant's surface was a sprawl of gleaming metal buildings and tall skyscrapers. Towering over them all was the Jedi Temple, a large structure topped with five spires, each one housing a sacred temple chamber.

The centre chamber was the home to the Jedi Council, comprised of twelve Jedi Masters who governed the order. Yoda, the Grand Master of the Council, and Mace Windu met in the council chamber to discuss an urgent problem. They needed to contact two of the best Jedi generals in the Republic Army: Obi-Wan Kenobi and Anakin Skywalker.

Getting in touch with the generals hadn't been easy. The Jedi were meant to be wrapping up a victory against the droid army on planet Christophsis. But all attempts to contact them on the planet had failed. Obi-Wan and Anakin had sent their fleet off to gather more supplies, so Windu and Yoda tried to communicate with the fleet's lead cruiser.

Admiral Yularen of the Galactic Republic received the transmission in the ship's hologram room. Electric-blue images of Mace Windu and Yoda wavered in front of him.

Mace Windu was tall and lean, with serious, dark eyes. 'We need to make contact with General Kenobi,' he told the admiral.

'We've been unable to reach him,' Yularen reported. 'It could be a solar storm, or maybe they are rebooting their communication system. I'm sure the blackout is temporary.'

Yoda nodded. He stood not even as high as Windu's waist, but the lines on his round face, which had taken almost nine hundred years to form, showed his strength and his wisdom. 'A messenger we are sending,' he said. 'With important orders for General Kenobi.'

'See to it that she gets there as fast as possible,' Windu added.

'Yes, sir,' Yularen replied. 'We will embark once we load the relief supplies.'

Yoda looked concerned. 'No time, there is. Immediately the messenger must go.'

The hologram faded. Admiral Yularen understood

the importance of the Jedi's request and prepared to launch a shuttle to the planet's surface.

Sending a messenger to the planet seemed an easy enough task, but unbeknownst to the admiral, the Jedi generals were experiencing much more than a communications glitch . . .

CHAPTER ONE

On planet Christophsis, laser cannon blasts
shattered the wall of a crystal skyscraper. Anakin
Skywalker shouted out a warning to his clone
troopers.

'They're back!' he announced.

Anakin and Obi-Wan Kenobi had been fighting
off small pockets of battle droids all over Crystal
City. They'd won their last skirmish, and a quiet calm
had fallen over the city. But their victory was short-
lived. Another droid platoon, the largest yet, was
heading their way.

'I told you that our victory was too easy,'
Obi-Wan said. 'We never should have sent the ship
back for supplies.'

'It wasn't my idea to send the ship back,' Anakin
protested.

The younger Jedi was proud and hated to admit when he'd made a mistake. Pride was a dangerous thing for a Jedi to have, but Obi-Wan resisted the urge to lecture his former student. This was not the time for a lesson in humility.

Obi-Wan turned to the small group of clone troopers that was gathering behind them. Each trooper looked identical in a suit of heavy-duty white armour that covered every inch of their skin. Each clone carried a DC-15 Blaster, a powerful plasma gun capable of blowing a droid to pieces with just one shot.

'All right, men. There is a second wave coming,' Obi-Wan warned.

Anakin pointed to one of the troopers. The blue armour plates on his shoulders, knees and helmet marked him as a clone captain.

'Rex, you and your men follow me!' Anakin ordered.

Anakin, clone Captain Rex and a small number of troopers ran to the side of the street, leaving Obi-Wan with the rest of the clone troopers. The remaining clones were led by clone Commander Cody.

As the droid platoon moved into range, the

troopers fanned out behind Obi-Wan. Battle droids, carrying blaster rifles, marched towards them in formation. Behind the battle droids marched lines of super battle droids, their dark grey, armoured bodies hulking above the battle droids. Instead of blaster rifles, each super battle droid had a built-in weapon: a double laser cannon on the end of its right arm.

Two dwarf spider droids flanked the other droids. Each of these droids had a large dome-shaped body with a centrally mounted laser cannon and two red lights on top that resembled sinister, glowing eyes. The spider droids marched forward on four long, jointed legs.

Unlike the clone troopers, the Jedi were not heavily armoured, and could outrun any droid that the Separatists could dream up. Obi-Wan wore boots and a light brown tunic over light armour that covered his chest and arms, and Anakin wore a dark tunic and boots. Instead of heavy blasters, they relied on their lightsabers, the Jedi's weapons of choice.

'Battle positions!' Obi-Wan shouted and waved at Cody and the clone troopers.

They charged ahead, running straight into the oncoming wave of droids. The air exploded with light and heat as the battle droids fired their weapons. The clone troopers kept charging; their armour protected them from most of the blasts. Obi-Wan shielded himself with the long, blue blade of his lightsaber. He expertly slashed his way through the oncoming droids, slicing through their metal bodies with ease.

Commander Cody fired at the droids with his DC-15. Droid after droid went down, but for every fallen droid another marched in to take its place.

'General Skywalker should have attacked by now!' Cody cried out.

'Don't worry!' Obi-Wan shouted back. 'He knows the plan!'

On the other side of the battlefield, Anakin was getting ready to make his move. He had led the troops around the droid offensive, and had scaled a tall energy sphere. He gazed down at the rear flanks of the droid army. The enemy had saved their most powerful droids for last. Three large octuptarra droids thundered down the streets. They resembled the spider droids, but were nearly twice as tall. The octuptarra stomped along on three tall legs. Their dome-shaped heads rotated 360 degrees, making them capable of firing in all directions.

'What's our plan of attack, sir?' one of the troopers asked.

Anakin grinned. 'Follow me.'

He leaped off the energy sphere, somersaulted in mid-air, and landed on top of one of the octuptarra droids. The startled droid spun its head quickly, trying to shake the Jedi free.

Another of the octuptarra droids spotted Anakin and fired. The Jedi deflected the attack with his lightsaber and then plunged the glowing blue blade straight down into the head of the droid he was standing on. The octuptarra fell hard. Anakin jumped off as the droid crashed to the ground. He raced ahead, followed closely by the clone troops.

It took a moment for the battle droids to realize they were being attacked from behind. They shot their blasters wildly, not sure where to aim. As Anakin's troops pressed forward, he jumped on top of the second octuptarra droid. Before he destroyed it, he looked out over the battlefield. He could see Obi-Wan and his troops surging ahead, wiping out every droid in their path. Their plan was working!

Anakin jumped off the octuptarra as it crashed to the ground. He landed on the third droid. It almost felt too easy. He quickly took down the final, massive droid with one blow from his lightsaber. He then jumped down and joined the fray.

Anakin and the clone troopers cut through the droids, working their way up from the rear. From the front, Obi-Wan led his soldiers and battled towards Anakin. In the middle, the two Jedi met. The bodies of fallen droids surrounded them, but their victory was short-lived: more droids were on their way.

'We're going to need reinforcements,' Anakin told Obi-Wan.

'We haven't been able to get through to the admiral,' Obi-Wan replied.

On the far side of the street, the battle droid captain talked to a hologram of General Whorm Loathsom, a leader in the Separatist cause. Unlike the droids, Loathsom was made of flesh and blood, but his appearance was just as disturbing. His blue, scaly head rose to a tall point above his hulking shoulders; tusk-like teeth stuck out of his narrow lower jaw.

'We cannot get past their cannons, sir,' the droid reported.

'This will never do,' Loathsom said angrily, in a voice as rough as Tatooine sand. 'We must pull back and set up our defence shields. Turn the troops around!'

The hologram disappeared and the droid captain shouted to his troops.

'Retreat! Retreat!'

The droids responded at once. 'Roger. Roger.' They immediately began to march back to their stronghold.

'They're pulling back,' Anakin realized.

He and Obi-Wan watched the droids retreat. Then they both noticed something else: a Republic attack shuttle flying overhead. The sleek white spacecraft with red markings was a welcome sight.

Obi-Wan was relieved. 'Looks like help has arrived!'

CHAPTER TWO

Obi-Wan and Anakin walked towards City Plaza, which they had commandeered as a landing site. Rex and some of the clone troopers followed behind. R2-D2, Anakin's astromech droid, rolled up as they approached. Artoo was smaller than a battle droid, and didn't come equipped with any blasting weapons, but the droid had helped Anakin out of many dangerous situations.

'Our cruiser must be back,' Obi-Wan guessed. 'This solves all of our problems. Fresh troops, new supplies, and perhaps they brought my new Padawan with them.'

'You really think it's a good idea to bring a Padawan learner into all this?' Anakin asked.

Obi-Wan nodded. 'I spoke to Master Yoda

about it. You should put in a request for one. You'd make a good teacher.'

Anakin chuckled. He was too busy fighting droids to babysit some young wannabe Jedi who didn't know one end of a lightsaber from the other. 'No thanks.'

Obi-Wan sighed. 'Anakin, teaching is a privilege. It's part of a Jedi's responsibility to help teach the next generation.'

'A Padawan would just slow me down,' Anakin replied.

They had arrived at the plaza. Giant laser cannons protected the perimeter. The shuttle touched down in the middle of the plaza. A ramp unfolded, and a small girl walked out.

'A youngling?' Obi-Wan wondered out loud. The girl was Togruta, from planet Shili. Like the rest of her people, the girl had skin the colour of red clay and white markings around her eyes and on her forehead. Because she was young, the white horns on top of her head were short, and her lekku had only just reached her shoulders. One of the head-tails grew down her back, and the other two grew down either side of her head. The lekku looked striking, with alternating stripes of white and bright blue.

The girl confidently marched up to the Jedi generals. She didn't seem fazed to have landed in the middle of a war zone.

'And who are you supposed to be?' Anakin asked rudely. Artoo scolded him with a beep.

The girl looked hurt, but only for a second. 'I'm Ahsoka,' she replied, confident once more. 'Master Yoda sent me. I was told to tell both of you that you must get back to the Jedi Temple immediately. There's an emergency.'

'Well, I don't know if you've noticed, but *we're* in a bit of an emergency right here,' Anakin snapped.

'Yes, our communications have been unreliable, but we've been calling for help,' Obi-Wan informed her.

'Master Yoda hadn't heard from you so he sent me to deliver the message,' Ahsoka explained.

Anakin shook his head. 'Great! They don't even know we're in trouble.'

Ahsoka unhooked a hologram comdisk from her belt. 'Maybe you can relay a signal through the cruiser that just dropped me off.'

Anakin wouldn't admit it out loud, but the

youngling's idea was a good one. Ahsoka used the comdisk to contact the cruiser. An image of the clone trooper at the cruiser's command centre appeared in front of them in the plaza and the Padawan explained their situation.

'We're under attack by Separatist warships, but I will try to make contact with the Jedi Temple for you,' the clone told them. 'Stand by.'

A moment later, a fuzzy hologram of Yoda appeared.

'Master Kenobi, glad Ahsoka found you, I am,' Yoda said.

'Master Yoda, we are trapped here, and vastly outnumbered,' Obi-Wan informed him. 'We are in no position to go anywhere or do anything. Our support ships have all been destroyed.'

'Send reinforcements to you, we will,' Yoda said.

Before the Jedi could respond, Yoda's image fizzled and faded out.

'Master Yoda? Master Yoda?' Obi-Wan called out.

A hologram of the Jedi cruiser captain appeared in Yoda's place. 'We've lost the transmission, sir.'

On the cruiser, Admiral Yularen approached the captain. 'We've got to leave orbit. More enemy ships have arrived.'

'We'll get back to you as soon as we can,' the captain told Obi-Wan.

The transmissions from the cruiser fizzled out for good.

Anakin sighed. 'I guess we'll have to hold out a little longer.'

Obi-Wan turned to Ahsoka. 'My apologies, young one. It's time for a proper introduction.'

'I'm the new Padawan learner, Ahsoka Tano,' the girl replied.

The older Jedi smiled. 'I'm Obi-Wan Kenobi, your new Master.'

Ahsoka bowed her head respectfully. 'I'm at your service, Master Kenobi, but I've actually been assigned to Master Skywalker.'

'What!' Anakin's blue eyes widened in surprise. 'No, no, no, no, no. There must be some mistake. *He's* the one who wanted the Padawan.'

'No, Master Yoda was very specific,' Ahsoka said. 'I am assigned to Anakin Skywalker and he is to supervise my Jedi training.'

Obi-Wan held up his hand. 'We'll have to sort this

out later. It won't be long before those droids figure out a way around our cannons.'

'I'll check with Rex on the lookout post,' Anakin said.

Obi-Wan looked right at him. 'You'd better take her with you.'

Anakin rolled his eyes and reluctantly motioned for Ahsoka to follow him. She quickly stepped behind him, smiling.

Anakin led her to an outpost on top of an abandoned crystal skyscraper. Clone troopers surrounded it, keeping an eye out for an enemy attack. They found Rex looking out over the city. The clone captain had his helmet off, revealing the strong features, brown eyes and brown hair typical of a clone trooper.

'What's the status, Rex?' Anakin asked.

'Quiet for now, sir. They're gearing up for another assault,' Rex reported. He nodded at Ahsoka. 'Who's the youngling?'

'I'm Master Skywalker's Padawan,' Ahsoka replied firmly. 'The name's Ahsoka Tano.'

Rex raised an eyebrow. Anakin could see he was amused. 'Sir, I thought you said you'd never have a Padawan?'

'There's been a mix-up,' Anakin said crossly. 'The youngling isn't with me.'

'Stop calling me that,' Ahsoka said. 'You're stuck with me, Skyguy.'

'What did you just call me?' Anakin shot back as Rex laughed. 'Don't get snippy with me, little one. You know, I don't even think you're old enough to be a Padawan.'

The comment stung. Anakin was right. She was fourteen, two years shy of the usual age when students graduated to Padawan. But she had advanced to Padawan just the same.

'Well, maybe I'm not, but Master Yoda thinks I am,' she replied, her dark eyes glittering with pride.

'Well, you're not with Master Yoda now. So if you're ready, you'd better start proving it,' Anakin said. He motioned towards Rex. 'Captain Rex is going to demonstrate how a little respect can go a long way.'

Rex slung his blaster rifle over his shoulder and headed for the stairs.

'Come on, youngling,' he ordered.

'*Padawan*,' Ahsoka mumbled under her breath. She glared at Anakin as she followed the clone leader.

Rex and Ahsoka made their way through the rubble in the city square. They walked past a line of clone troopers manning heavy artillery.

'Have you thought about moving that line back, Captain?' Ahsoka suggested. 'They'd have better cover that way.'

'Thanks for the suggestion, but General Skywalker thinks they're fine where they are,' Rex replied.

Ahsoka was thoughtful for a moment. 'So if you're a captain, and I'm a Jedi, then technically, I outrank you, right?'

Rex didn't like that idea. 'But technically, you're only a youngling,' he pointed out.

'Padawan!' Ahsoka corrected him.

Rex shrugged. 'Either way. In my book, experience outranks everything.'

'Well, if experience outranks everything, I guess I'd better start getting some,' Ahsoka pointed out.

Rex smiled, admiring her spirit. Ahsoka smiled back. Then, suddenly, a giant dome of glowing, orange-red energy appeared on the other edge of the city.

'What's that?' Ahsoka asked.

Rex's smile faded. 'Not good. They've got an

energy shield. It'll be nearly impossible to hold back their attack.'

As he spoke, the dome began to expand, spreading closer to City Plaza.

'If you want experience, little one, it looks like you're about to get plenty,' Rex said.

Ahsoka looked at the glowing shield. Doubt flashed across her mind. *Was* she ready for this?

She quickly shook away the thought. Master Yoda thought she was ready. She wouldn't fail him.

Most of all, she wanted to show Master Skywalker what she could do.

CHAPTER THREE

Anakin, Obi-Wan, Rex and Ahsoka gathered inside the communication station the generals had set up in Crystal City. They studied a large hologram map that showed the city's layout. Massive droid armies were gathering all over town, getting closer to the Republic's stronghold.

Obi-Wan pointed to a spot on the map. 'The shield generator's somewhere in here. They're slowly increasing the diameter of the energy shield, and keeping it just ahead of their troops.'

'Artillery's going to be useless against that,' Rex said.

Obi-Wan thoughtfully stroked his beard. 'As they get closer, I suppose we could try to draw them into the buildings. That might level the playing field a bit.'

Ahsoka spoke up. 'If that shield's gonna be such a problem, why don't we just take it out?'

The three men gave her a weary look.

'Easier said than done,' Rex grumbled.

'I, for one, agree with her,' Anakin said. Ahsoka couldn't believe it. Obi-Wan and Rex looked at Anakin in surprise.

'Someone has to get to that shield generator and destroy it,' Anakin went on. 'That's the key.'

'Right, then,' Obi-Wan agreed. 'Maybe you two can tiptoe through enemy lines and solve this particular problem together.'

Ahsoka felt like cheering. She was going on a real Jedi mission, and an important one, at that. 'Can do, Master Kenobi!'

'I'll decide what we do,' Anakin told her.

Obi-Wan pointed to the map again. 'If Rex and I can engage them here, you two might have a chance to get through their lines, undetected, there.'

'They won't have much time,' Rex warned. 'The droids far outnumber us, so our ability to fight is limited without the use of artillery. If the shield continues to expand, the droids will be able to get close enough to destroy our heavy cannons. Without those cannons, we're helpless.'

'We'll figure out a way!' Ahsoka said confidently. She tugged at Anakin's sleeve. 'Come on, Master, let's go!'

Anakin shook his head. 'If we survive this, Snips, you and I are gonna have a talk.'

They left the communication station and made their way through the rubble in the streets until they found a burned-out skyscraper with a good view of the droid shield. They climbed twenty storeys to the top and Anakin surveyed the scene with his macrobinoculars. In the distance, the droid army marched towards them, protected by the energy shield.

'So, what's the plan?' Ahsoka asked eagerly.

Anakin lowered the binoculars. 'Oh, I thought *you* were the one with the plan.'

'No, *I'm* the one with the enthusiasm,' the Padawan responded. 'You're the one with the experience, which I'm looking forward to learning from.'

'Well, first we need to get behind that shield, then get behind their tank lines,' Anakin said.

'Why don't we just go around the shield?' Ahsoka asked.

'That'd take too long,' Anakin replied.

'Sneak through the middle, then?' Ahsoka suggested.

'Impossible. Unless you want to turn yourself into a droid.'

Ahsoka threw up her hands. 'All right, you win! My first lesson will be to wait while you come up with the answer.'

A slight smile crossed Anakin's face. Talking with Ahsoka had given him an idea.

'Well, the wait's over,' he said. 'I've got a plan.'

Back at City Plaza, Obi-Wan and Rex stood near the Republic laser cannons. If anything could blast through that shield, it would be the powerful cannons.

At Obi-Wan's signal, the cannons fired.

BOOM! BOOM! BOOM! BOOM!

Obi-Wan and Rex watched, hopeful, as the fire from the cannons impacted the glowing shield, but the powerful blasts didn't damage the shield at all. And when the smoke cleared, the men saw an even more disturbing sight: a line of droid tanks rolling in behind the battle droids. Obi-Wan knew the tanks were armed with ion cannons as well as laser cannons, both easily capable of destroying the Republic's artillery.

Obi-Wan sighed. 'That shield is certainly putting a crimp in my day.'

'It's no use, sir. Even at full power, our cannons can't take down that shield,' Rex said.

'It was worth a try,' Obi-Wan said. 'Tell the men to fall back.'

While Obi-Wan and the troopers retreated, Anakin and Ahsoka carried out Anakin's plan. Anakin had spotted a lightweight piece of rubble that resembled a big trunk. He and Ahsoka crawled underneath it, and shuffled towards the shield on their hands and knees. Anakin wore a satchel around his neck; it contained the explosive charges they would need to complete their mission.

'This is a stupid plan!' Ahsoka complained. 'We should fight these guys, instead of sneaking around.'

'My stupid plan is working,' Anakin replied. 'We passed under the shield meters some time ago, without being detected.'

'If you say so,' Ahsoka mumbled.

Anakin stopped suddenly. 'Wait. Hear that?'

A low rumbling sound was getting louder by the second, and the ground beneath them began to vibrate. Anakin lifted the trunk so they could see what was coming.

Ahsoka gasped. Separatist tank droids filled the entire street in front of them. They were about to be crushed!

CHAPTER FOUR

'Get out, quick!' Anakin yelled.

He ran out from under the trunk. Ahsoka let out
a cry and ran to the right, away from Anakin. A tank
rolled right between them.

Anakin ran behind the tank, trying to reach
Ahsoka. But she had to move to the left to avoid
another tank.

'Get back here!' Anakin yelled.

Ahsoka rolled on the ground as another tank
approached. 'I'm trying!'

Anakin quickly made his way through the rolling
maze of tank treads, trying to reach Ahsoka. As he
got close, one of the tanks was almost on top of her.
He quickly reached out and grabbed her, pulling her
to the side. Together, they reached the end of the line
of tanks. The trunk had made it safely to the side,

too. Anakin pulled the trunk over them both.

Ahsoka's heart was pounding. They had made it, but it had been close.

Back on the battle-strewn streets, Obi-Wan and Rex watched the advancing droid army from the safety of the communication station.

'They're entering the city,' Rex said.

'Try to draw them into the buildings,' Obi-Wan ordered. 'Stay inside until the shield passes over. The tanks will have a hard time manoeuvring. Then we'll see what damage we can do.'

'Yes, sir!' Rex signalled the troopers to get ready.

The droid army advanced quickly. This time, super battle droids took the front lines. They quickly targeted the comm station, rocking the building with powerful laser blasts.

The super battle droids crashed through the crumbling walls, attacking the clone troopers at close range. One of the droids picked up a trooper by the throat and Obi-Wan leaped into the fray, slashing off the droid's arm with his lightsaber.

The injured clone trooper fell to the ground. Obi-Wan knelt down to help him as the one-armed droid advanced again. Obi-Wan held out his hand

and pushed the droid away using the power of the Force.

The super battle droid hovered in the air for a second before it was hit with a shot from a blaster bolt. The droid exploded into pieces. Obi-Wan looked to see where the shot had come from and saw Rex standing there.

'We're inside the shield now,' Obi-Wan said. 'If we stay away from those tanks, we should be okay.'

'We're not going to be able to stop them from reaching the heavy cannons,' Rex warned.

Obi-Wan knew what had to be done. 'Move your troops back to the heavy cannons. Do everything you can do to protect them. I'll delay the droids.'

'But . . .' Rex couldn't just leave his general at the mercy of the entire droid army.

Obi-Wan was firm. 'That is an order, Captain!'

Rex reluctantly led his troops away from the comm station. Another super battle droid appeared around a corner. It lifted an arm, aiming its double laser cannons at Obi-Wan.

Whoosh! Obi-Wan ignited his lightsaber and with a swift slice, he knocked the droid to the ground. The Jedi jumped out of the comm station into the street and began slashing battle droids.

BAM! A huge explosion rocked the ground. Obi-Wan looked up to see the first tank crashing through the rubble. He shook his head. 'I hope Anakin and Ahsoka get to that shield generator soon.'

On the other side of the battle, Anakin and Ahsoka watched the last tank roll away.

'I think we made it past all of them, Master,' Ahsoka said. 'We may pull this off yet.'

'We still have a long way to go before we get to the generator station,' Anakin reminded her.

Ahsoka tapped the side of the trunk. 'Do we still need this thing? I can't take it any more. I have to stand up.'

'You've got to be careful,' Anakin warned. 'You never know what you're going to run into.'

Suddenly, they hit something with a loud smack. The impact knocked them both to the ground.

A destroyer droid was right in front of them, unrolling from its ball shape to unleash the twin blasters at the end of its arms. At its full height, the bronze droid looked like some kind of giant metallic insect.

'See what I mean?' Anakin quipped.

Ahsoka gripped her lightsaber, but she knew it would be useless against a destroyer droid. Its built-in generators equipped the droid with a strong protective shield.

She and Anakin quickly stepped backwards as the droid began firing rapidly.

'Run!' Anakin yelled.

'What? Jedi don't run!' Ahsoka replied.

'I said RUN!'

Ahsoka and Anakin turned and ran down the street, deflecting laser bolts with their lightsabers as they ran. Seeing its attack fail, the droid transformed back into its wheel form and began rolling after them.

'Stop!' Anakin called out.

'Make up your mind,' Ahsoka shot back.

Anakin stopped short. 'I said stop!'

Ahsoka obeyed, and then the two raced back to meet the droid as it rolled towards them. Before it could unravel again, they activated their lightsabers. Ahsoka's weapon shimmered with green energy.

Slash! They cut the droid in two.

'Good,' Anakin said. 'You take direction well.'

Ahsoka smiled. Anakin had gone from wishing she didn't exist to praising her in one afternoon.

Anakin looked up at the shield, studying it. The

orange glow was more intense in one area of the sky. Without a word, Anakin ran towards it, and Ahsoka quickly followed.

They soon came to an open field littered with the shells of bombed-out buildings. A shield generator had been erected in the field's centre.

'There it is!' Ahsoka cried. 'Come on!'

'Stay close,' Anakin instructed. 'We've got to be careful.'

In her excitement to reach the generator, Ahsoka ignored him. 'We're almost there.'

'I said wait!' Anakin yelled.

Ahsoka reached the edge of the field. In the corner of her eye, she noticed several antennas sticking up from the ground. Too late, she realized why Anakin had tried to stop her.

She tried to come to a halt, but lost her balance. She stepped backwards, and her right foot landed on one of the antennas. Behind her, Anakin winced.

A loud alarm went off, and a hidden army of droids began to emerge from under the earth, like zombies rising from the grave.

'Oops,' Ahsoka said.

'Forget about the droids,' Anakin said, throwing her the satchel. 'Set the charges!'

'Right!' Ahsoka said. She caught the satchel in one hand and sliced off the head of an orange retail droid with the other. The droid rolled backwards over another row of antennas on the field.

The motion awakened even more retail droids. They broke through the ground and headed right for Anakin.

'Sorry!' Ahsoka called out.

'Whose side are you on, anyway?' Anakin cried, slicing through a droid with his lightsaber. 'Just finish with those charges!'

'Setting the charges,' Ahsoka repeated. She ran across the field, making sure to dodge the antennas.

Back at the comm station, Obi-Wan fought valiantly against the battle droids. But there were just too many to defeat, even for a great Jedi Knight.

A giant tank rolled to a stop inside the comm station. The hatch opened, and General Loathsom's big blue head appeared.

'You must be the infamous General Kenobi,' Loathsom said, his snout curled in a victorious grin.

Obi-Wan raised his hands in the air. 'I give up,' he said. 'I surrender!'

CHAPTER FIVE

General Loathsom ordered his super battle droids to surround Obi-Wan. The general climbed out of the tank and one of the battle droids confiscated Obi-Wan's lightsaber.

Like any good general, Obi-Wan had studied his enemy. Loathsom was notorious for being as vain as he was cruel and Obi-Wan hoped that he could use that to his advantage.

Obi-Wan picked up a table that had been overturned by the explosions, set it upright, and then put a chair on either side of it. Loathsom watched in confusion as Obi-Wan sat in one chair, and indicated for him to sit in the other.

'Don't try any of your tricks, Jedi,' Loathsom growled.

'General? If you please?' Obi-Wan asked, still pointing at the chair.

'Have you gone mad?' Loathsom bellowed.

'Not at all,' Obi-Wan replied calmly. 'I've conceded the battle. Now we simply have to negotiate the terms of surrender.'

Loathsom looked at him sceptically, but Obi-Wan could see he had the general's attention.

'Surely there's no reason we can't be civilized about this,' Obi-Wan said, his voice as smooth as butter.

Loathsom took the bait. He could be just as civilized as any mere *human*.

'Yes, of course,' he replied. He straightened his uniform and took a seat at the table.

'It's a rare honour to be able to meet one's opponent face-to-face,' Obi-Wan said. 'You're a legend throughout the Inner Core.'

Loathsom beamed. 'Thank you. The honour is all mine. I'm so glad you decided to surrender rather than to fight this out to the bitter end.'

'Well, at some point, we must accept the reality of the situation,' Obi-Wan said cheerfully. 'Might we have some refreshments?'

*

Anakin slashed away at the orange retail droids while Ahsoka scurried around the shield generator, sticking grapefruit-sized explosive charges to its surface. She flipped a switch on the last one as she placed it on to a control panel. All of the charges began to blink and beep. Satisfied, she jumped off the generator, ignited her lightsaber, and ran to join Anakin.

The droids had surrounded the Jedi, and backed him up against a single, large crumbling wall that had once been part of a building. Ahsoka thrust her lightsaber at one of the droids and examined the wall. There was one open window several storeys up. She looked down at Anakin and back up at the window as she formed an idea.

'Skyguy, don't move!' Ahsoka called out.

'What?' Anakin replied.

Ahsoka extended a hand towards the wall. Like other young Jedi, she had been trained in the use of the Force at the Jedi Temple. She had never moved anything as large as the wall . . . yet.

Anakin saw what she was trying to do.

'No, no, no!' he yelled.

Ahsoka became one with the Force and focused all of her will on the wall. It came crumbling down,

crushing the orange retail droids below it. But
Anakin stood there, untouched, just as Ahsoka had
planned. The window had fallen right around him,
keeping him safe.

Anakin was furious. He pointed at Ahsoka. 'You
could have gotten me killed!'

Obi-Wan slowly sipped a cup of tea that Loathsom's
servant droid had brought him. He talked and talked,
trying to stall for time.

'And of course, once you've taken custody of
my troops, arrangements will need to be made for
their food and shelter. Tell me, do you have enough
supplies to –'

'Enough of this!' Loathsom fumed, pounding a
clawed fist on the table. 'You are stalling!'

'Nonsense!' Obi-Wan replied. 'General, there are
numerous details to discuss.'

Loathsom growled and stood up, knocking the
table to the side. 'Seize him!'

Two orange retail droids grabbed Obi-Wan, lifting
him from the ground.

'Unless you call off your troops right now, I
will have no choice but to destroy you,' Loathsom
threatened.

'Truthfully, I was hoping your shield would be knocked out by now, but since it isn't, I suppose I have to move to Plan B,' Obi-Wan said calmly.

In the blink of an eye, the Jedi flipped himself into the air, somersaulting over the retail droids. He landed behind them, and then channelled the power of the Force to smash the machines into each other.

He jumped behind General Loathsom and put his neck in a choke hold. The droids backed up, not sure if they should fire at the Jedi and risk hitting their general, too.

Anakin and Ahsoka were still arguing at the shield generator.

'I know what I'm doing,' Ahsoka said.

'I had everything under control. I didn't need your help,' Anakin said.

Ahsoka couldn't believe his attitude. 'I just saved your life!'

Then Anakin came to his senses. They had more important things to do than argue.

'Did you get the charges set?' Anakin asked.

'Yes,' Ahsoka replied.

'Then what are you waiting for?' Anakin asked.

Ahsoka nodded and pressed the detonator.

KA-BOOM! The charges exploded at once, destroying the shield generator with one massive blast. The orange shield in the sky slowly fizzled out.

Over at the comm station, Obi-Wan looked at the sky and grinned.

'Ah, something appears to have happened to your shield, General,' he said.

Loathsom groaned, and his battle droids looked at one another, confused.

A hologram of Admiral Yularen appeared on the comm station's console.

'General Kenobi, if you can hear me, we're through the blockade,' he reported. 'The Separatist armada is in retreat. Your reinforcements should be landing in a moment.'

Obi-Wan looked outside the station to see Republic cruisers and fighters landing in the distance. Jedi gunships flew by, chasing the droid army as they made a hasty retreat.

'It's all over now, General,' Obi-Wan told Loathsom, who was still trapped in a headlock. 'Now it's my turn to negotiate the treaty. Tell your troops to lay down their arms.'

'Surrender! Surrender!' Loathsom cried.

CHAPTER SIX

Ahsoka slumped down on to the field and lowered her head. Taking down the shield generator felt great, but a feeling of dread came over her as the events of the day sank in. It was her fault that the retail droids had been activated. And even though her move had saved Anakin, it had made him furious. She wondered if he was planning on sending her back to the Jedi Temple.

Anakin sat down next to her. 'You're reckless, little one,' he said. 'You never would have made it as Obi-Wan's Padawan, but you might make it as mine.'

Ahsoka looked up at him, a hopeful grin on her face. Anakin smiled back at her.

The unmistakable whirr of a spacecraft filled

the field. They both looked up to see a Jedi gunship landing next to them. The hatch opened, and Rex reached out to pull Anakin and Ahsoka on board.

'Great job, General Skywalker,' he said. He nodded at Ahsoka. 'You, too, kid.'

They flew into the planet's orbit and landed on the loading ramp of a Jedi cruiser. As they stepped out on to the deck, they saw Obi-Wan standing there next to Yoda. Anakin and Ahsoka walked over to the two Jedi Masters and bowed.

'Master Obi-Wan. Master Yoda,' Anakin greeted them.

'Hmmm,' Yoda said, eyeing Ahsoka. 'Trouble you have with your new Padawan, I hear.'

Ahsoka gave Anakin a worried look. Was she in trouble after all?

'I was just explaining the situation to Master Yoda,' Obi-Wan said.

Yoda looked at Anakin. 'If not ready for a Padawan you are, then perhaps Obi-Wan can –'

'Now wait a minute!' Anakin interrupted. 'I admit Ahsoka's a little rough around the edges. But with a great deal of training and patience, she might amount to something.'

Ahsoka smiled at Anakin's kindness. Obi-Wan

and Yoda shared a look. Anakin's reaction was just what they had hoped.

'Then go with you, she will, to the Teth system,' Yoda said.

'Teth? That's wild space,' Anakin said, confused. 'The droid army isn't even in that sector.'

'Kidnapped, Jabba the Hutt's son has been,' Yoda explained.

Anakin held back a groan. Jabba was a low-down gangster who smelled like a rotting tauntaun carcass to boot. 'You want me to rescue Jabba's son?'

'Anakin, we'll need the Hutt's allegiance to give us an advantage over Dooku,' Obi-Wan said.

Anakin's face clouded at the mention of Count Dooku's name. The former Jedi had turned his back on all of his training, choosing the dark side of the Force. Obi-Wan and Anakin had battled him, and Anakin had paid a great price: the loss of his right arm. The new mechanical one worked just as well as his old one had, but a spark of anger against Dooku still burned in Anakin's heart.

'Negotiate the treaty with Jabba, Obi-Wan will. Find the renegades that hold Jabba's son your mission will be, Skywalker,' Yoda instructed.

Anakin was not enthusiastic, but Ahsoka was

happy. Saving a kid from kidnappers was an exciting mission, even if the kid was slimy and smelly.

'Come on, Master, it doesn't sound that hard,' Ahsoka urged. 'I'll find Rex and get the troops organized.'

The Jedi looked on as she ran off to get the soldiers.

'Don't worry, Anakin,' Obi-Wan said. 'Just teach her everything I taught you and she'll turn out fine.'

'You know, something makes me think this was your idea from the start,' Anakin said to his former Master.

Obi-Wan didn't respond, but he didn't have to: Anakin saw the answer in his eyes.

Anakin smiled, shook his head and hopped into his gunship. It might not be the most pleasant challenge, but he was a Jedi and ready to take it on.

Besides, now he had help, thanks to his new Padawan.

CHAPTER SEVEN

Planet Tatooine sat in the Outer Rim, a lonely stretch of the galaxy that even the Republic didn't bother to deal with. Twin yellow suns shone on the desert planet, and the days were blazing hot and the nights were freezing cold.

The tallest building on Tatooine was Hutt Castle, a thick structure of sandblasted metal and pitted stone. The palace of greedy, seedy crime lord Jabba the Hutt was no place for a Jedi, yet Obi-Wan found himself there just the same.

Master Yoda had sent him to Jabba to negotiate a treaty with the Republic. They would find Jabba's kidnapped son, and in return, Jabba would grant the Republic safe passage through Hutt Space.

Obi-Wan carefully explained the deal through Jabba's protocol droid, TC-70. The bronze-coloured droid had the humanoid appearance of most protocol droids. With round, glowing eyes, it had a look of constant surprise.

'We will not let you down,' Obi-Wan finished.

He stood in Jabba's throne room. Obi-Wan had seen many terrible things in the galaxy, but it was still difficult to look at Jabba for a long period of time. The gangster looked like some kind of giant slug, with a huge head, gaping mouth and a wrinkled, slimy body that ended in a legless tail. Jabba's yellow reptilian eyes stared coldly at Obi-Wan.

'AHHH . . . WOWOGA SLEEMO MAKA PEEDUNKEE MUFKIN,' Jabba replied.

TC-70 translated. 'The most gracious Jabba has one more small condition. He demands you bring back the slime who kidnapped his little . . . punky muffin.'

Obi-Wan tried not to smile. 'Punky . . .?'

'NEECHOOTU TAWNTEE SABEESKA!' Jabba bellowed.

'Dead or alive,' TC-70 informed Obi-Wan.

'OH. WOTOKI KA ROTTA, DOOKU DROI SEPARAHTEE WAN,' Jabba said, waving his stubby hands.

The protocol droid fixed his eyes on Obi-Wan.

'If you do not succeed, Count Dooku and his droid army will.'

Obi-Wan bowed to Jabba and retreated from the throne room. It was all up to Anakin and Ahsoka now. They had taken Rex, a small army of clone troopers and five gunships aboard a Jedi transport. It was believed that Jabba's son, Rotta, had been taken to planet Teth, another world in the Outer Rim. The transport had just established orbit over Teth. The five gunships descended from the hangar bay as gracefully as birds in flight, diving into the purple clouds of dawn.

Obi-Wan contacted Anakin, who was commanding the lead gunship. Anakin and Ahsoka watched the hologram of the Jedi general as Obi-Wan delivered his message.

'Here's the story,' Obi-Wan began. 'Jabba has given us only one planetary rotation to get his son back to Tatooine safe and sound.'

'It won't take that long, Master,' Anakin assured him.

'Well, take extreme care,' Obi-Wan cautioned. 'We have no idea who is holding Jabba's son. When I've finished negotiations with him, I will join you.'

Anakin grinned. 'Who needs help? I've got Ahsoka with me.'

Obi-Wan winked at Anakin. 'Well then, perhaps she can keep you out of trouble.'

Ahsoka smiled as the hologram of Obi-Wan disappeared. The young Padawan walked to the window of the gunship and gazed down at the planet below. A thick jungle stretched out below them, covered in mist. In the distance, she could see a tall palace on top of a high rock mesa. This was their destination: an abandoned Hutt castle. The squad of gunships moved into formation. The plan was simple: land, storm the castle, rescue Rotta, and get back to Tatooine.

Anakin walked up next to Ahsoka. He could see in her eyes that she was ready for whatever lay ahead.

'Stay close to me, if you can,' he told her.

'It won't be a problem, Master,' Ahsoka replied.

Anakin frowned. Confidence was good, but being *too* confident could be dangerous. 'This isn't practice,' he reminded her.

Ahsoka looked up at him. 'I know. I'll try not to get you killed.'

Anakin was about to make a witty comeback when . . . *BOOM*! A round of laser fire blasted the gunship. Through the window, they could see a hail of blazing bolts rocketing towards the gunships.

Hawk, the ship's clone pilot, called out from his post. 'Sir! We're taking heavy fire!'

'Close the blast shields, Lieutenant!' Anakin ordered. 'Get us under those guns!'

'Yes, sir!' Hawk replied.

Armour slid over the windows, throwing the cabin into darkness. The emergency lighting activated, bathing everyone in red light.

Bam! Bam! Bam! More laser blasts slammed against the armour. The ship bounced with each impact.

So this won't be as easy as we thought, Ahsoka realized. She closed her eyes, centring herself.

'Here we go,' she whispered.

The clone troopers readied their blasters.

'Troops, stand by!' Rex yelled.

They gathered at the door, ready to leave the ship. The five gunships dropped at the same time, sailing below the trees of the jungle.

'Welcome to paradise, rockjumpers,' Hawk joked.

The five ships landed. Their doors flew open at once as the troopers poured out, rushing into the jungle.

'Green light! Go! Go! Go!' Rex yelled.

Anakin and Ahsoka followed the troopers along the jungle floor. They soon arrived at the bottom of a tall rock mesa covered with vines. Hutt Castle loomed over them on top of the rock wall.

Ahsoka looked up at the castle in awe. Then a bright light blinded her.

Boom! Boom! Boom! Blast after blast of laser fire rained down from the top of the mesa. They were under attack!

CHAPTER EIGHT

Ahsoka quickly ignited her lightsaber to block the oncoming lasers from a line of battle droids on top of the castle wall. The battle droid commander shouted orders in a robotic voice.

'Concentrate fire on sector 11374265!'

The sergeant tried to repeat the order. '113– what was that again?'

The commander pointed. 'Just fire down there!'

The droids might not have been smart, but their position on top of the mesa gave them an advantage. Down at the bottom, Anakin had his own advantage: a small fleet of huge AT-TE walkers. The All Terrain Tactical Enforcers were big tanks that walked on six legs, armed with four powerful laser cannons. The AT-TE fired up at the wall, blasting a battle droid from its position. The droid plummeted to the ground.

Anakin spotted a rock ledge at the base of the mesa. He motioned to the troops. 'Follow me!'

They ran to the overhang and took cover underneath. The droid's lasers blasted at the ground around them. But they couldn't stay there forever.

'So . . . this is where the fun begins,' Ahsoka quipped.

Anakin grinned. 'Race ya to the top!'

'I'll give you a head start,' Ahsoka said.

Anakin shrugged. 'Your mistake!'

He quickly ran out from under the ledge, grabbed a vine, and started to climb up the side of the wall. Rex addressed the clone troopers.

'Ascension cables!'

The troopers aimed their blasters at the top of the mesa. Suspension cables fired from grapple launchers beneath the blaster barrels. The grappling hooks latched on to the top of the rock wall, and the cables quickly pulled the troopers up the steep sides.

'I'm right behind you, Master!' Ahsoka called up. She grabbed a vine and started to climb. An AT-TE walker began to stomp up the mesa beside her.

A determined look appeared on Ahsoka's face. She leaped on to the back of the walker and hitched a ride.

The battle droid commander spotted the advancing tanks.

'Target those walkers!' the droid commanded.

Immediately, two dwarf spider droids crawled down the wall, firing laserbolts at the walkers. The assault sent one AT-TE plummeting off the mesa.

BOOM! It exploded on the ground below.

The clone troopers fired back as they climbed up the rock face. A droid tumbled down the wall just past Anakin. He reached out with his lightsaber, chopping it in half.

Ahsoka climbed over the body of the AT-TE, positioning herself in front. She used her lightsaber to deflect the bolts from above. One shot got past her, hitting the gunner of the AT-TE. He fell out of his chair with a loud cry.

Ahsoka steadied herself. Without the gunner, she had no offence. All she could do was defend against the attack. She made sure to keep her lightsaber in front of her, protecting her body. Soon they would reach the top, and the battle would be on equal ground.

But the droids didn't want that to happen. A loud *ZOOM* filled the air as four battle droids on STAP fighters came flying along the wall. Each Single

Trooper Aerial Platform was equipped with a pair of blaster cannons. The droids stood upright as they piloted the flying weapons.

All four STAPs headed straight for Ahsoka's tank. They aimed a barrage of fire at the walker's feet. The AT-TE lurched, losing its grip. Ahsoka couldn't hold on. She tumbled over, falling off the side.

Her heart jumped in her body as she caught herself just in time, hanging on with one hand. She scrambled to climb back on to the front of the walker's body, but couldn't gain balance on the violently rocking vehicle.

The STAP fighters swung back around, ready to finish her off. Anakin raced down the wall and jumped on top of the tank. Then he bounded over Ahsoka's head. She watched, amazed, as the Jedi seemed to float in mid-air.

Anakin landed right on a STAP and steered it into another one, destroying them both. Then he jumped on to the third STAP and kicked off the droid pilot. He steered the STAP up the face of the mesa, firing at droids as he flew. He whizzed past Ahsoka and grinned.

'Gotta keep up!' he challenged.

'No fair!' Ahsoka called back. She frowned and climbed back on top of the tank.

Anakin blasted his way up the side of the mesa, aiming his attack at the spider droids. He cleared a path for Rex and the troopers to follow.

Ahsoka banged on the window of the AT-TE. 'Get this thing moving!' she shouted to the clone trooper inside.

Anakin reached the top of the rock wall. He jumped off the battered STAP. A group of battle droids immediately surrounded them.

'Surrender, Jedi!' the droid commander ordered.

Anakin ignited his lightsaber. He waded into the crowd of droids, slashing at them left and right. Soon the ground was littered with broken droids.

But Anakin had no time to rest. Three destroyer droids rolled up. Anakin grimaced.

'Blast it, Ahsoka,' he muttered. 'I told you to stay close to me.'

The destroyer droids began to unfold, about to attack. Then, from out of nowhere, a huge laser blast slammed into the destroyers. The three droids exploded into pieces.

Anakin turned to see Ahsoka in the gunner's chair

of the AT-TE. Smoke poured from the cannon's barrels.

'I can't get much closer, Skyguy,' Ahsoka said.

Anakin smiled up at her. 'I knew you'd get here, Snips, eventually.'

'Always in time to save your life,' Ahsoka teased.

Rex walked up to them. 'All clear, General,' he reported.

Anakin and Ahsoka surveyed the landscape of fallen droids. High up in the castle, a mysterious cloaked figure watched – and smiled.

Everything was going according to plan.

CHAPTER NINE

A gunship landed on the top of the mesa, next to the castle. Anakin and Ahsoka examined the droids they had just defeated. A big question hung in the air: what were Separatist droids doing all the way out here?

'There are too many droids here for them to be renegades,' Anakin reasoned. 'I sense Count Dooku's hand in this. Let's find Jabba's son and get out of here.'

'No problem. The hard part is over,' Ahsoka said.

Anakin looked up at the imposing castle. 'I wish you wouldn't say that.'

Anakin, Ahsoka and Rex formed a plan. They left most of the clone troopers outside the castle in case of another attack. Then the three of them took four clones with them into the castle. The armoured door guarding the entryway opened easily. It led into a long, dark tunnel. The walls on each side of the tunnel held recessed alcoves, each one capable of holding a possible threat. The clones turned on their helmet headlights, illuminating the space, and they moved forward.

'I don't like this place,' Rex said after they had gone a short way. 'It gives me the creeps.'

'This looks like one of those monk monasteries that I read about in my studies at the Temple,' Ahsoka remarked.

'Smugglers like Jabba take these monasteries over and turn them into their own personal retreats,' Anakin explained.

'And the monks just let them?' Ahsoka asked.

'Smugglers usually get what they want, one way or another,' Anakin said bitterly. He had spent a big part of his childhood enslaved by a Hutt; it was one of many memories he didn't like to talk about.

Suddenly, a droid appeared out of the gloom in front of them. The skinny silver droid had a humanoid body, but large, insect-like eyes. Anakin ignited his lightsaber. He could see a downward-leading staircase behind the droid.

'Uh, good guy or bad guy, Master?' Ahsoka asked.

Anakin nodded at the droid. 'Who are you?'

'Merely the humble caretaker, oh mighty sir,' the droid replied. 'You have liberated me from those dreadful battle bots. I am most thankful.'

'Where is the Hutt?' Anakin asked.

'The battle bots kept their prisoners on the detention level. I must warn you it is very dangerous down there, my friend,' the droid replied. He pointed a metal finger at Ahsoka. 'No place for a servant girl.'

Ahsoka whipped out her lightsaber. The green blade shone in the dark.

'Do servant girls carry these?' she asked. 'I am a Jedi Knight . . . or soon will be.'

The droid gave a stiff little bow. 'A thousand apologies, young one.'

Her pride stung, Ahsoka marched ahead. Anakin turned to Rex.

'Captain, we'll get the Hutt,' he instructed. 'Stay here and keep your eyes open.'

'Copy that, sir,' Rex replied.

The droid's big eyes followed Anakin and Ahsoka as they walked down the stairs. Rex watched the droid with suspicion. Did he see a sinister gleam there?

Probably just a reflection off my helmet light, Rex reassured himself. But he steadied his blaster just the same.

There was nothing to do but wait.

While Anakin and Ahsoka made their way to the detention chamber, a hooded figure strode into a secret room in the castle. A small troop of super battle droids crowded the chamber; they parted as the woman entered. A pair of lightsabers swung from her belt.

Asajj Ventress lowered the hood of her cloak, revealing a smooth, hairless head tattooed with thick black lines. Her severe appearance was designed to strike fear into the hearts of those who tried to oppose her: fitting for a disciple of the dark side of the Force.

From the folds in her cloak she produced a holoprojector and pressed a button. A hologram of Count Dooku appeared.

'They have taken the monastery, Master,' she reported. 'Skywalker is here. He's on his way to rescue the Hutt.'

'Well done, Ventress,' Dooku praised. 'All is going according to plan.'

'I could easily take them now,' Ventress offered. She had little interest in Dooku's plan, except as a way to get her close to Anakin Skywalker. She had almost killed the pompous Jedi once, and was eager to finish the job.

'Patience,' Dooku advised. 'Collect the data I need. You will get the chance at revenge soon enough.'

The hologram faded. A battle droid approached Ventress.

'Mistress, the Jedi have entered the dungeon.'

In the lowest regions of the castle, Anakin and Ahsoka walked through the maze-like corridors of the castle dungeon. From the corner of her eye, Ahsoka could see two battle droids hiding in the corners, waiting for the right moment to attack.

'Master, you know you're walking us into a trap,' Ahsoka said.

'I know,' Anakin replied.

'We just passed two more droids,' Ahsoka pointed out. Had her Master missed them?

'I know,' the Jedi repeated.

'Well, I don't like this,' Ahsoka said. 'Can I just take care of them?'

Anakin shrugged. 'If you feel so strongly about it, go ahead.'

Ahsoka quickly spun around, igniting her lightsaber as she moved.

Whoosh! Whoosh! She sliced the battle droids' blasters right out of their metal hands. Before they could react, she slashed each droid in half.

'Not bad,' Anakin said. 'You remembered to destroy their weapons first.'

'I'm improving on your technique,' Ahsoka said.

A third droid sprang out from behind the next doorway. Anakin quickly sliced through it with his lightsaber. He grinned at Ahsoka.

'Of course, you did miss one,' he pointed out.

The Padawan didn't let it faze her. 'I did that on purpose.'

As they approached the door to the next cell, Anakin held out his arm. 'I sense our kidnapped Hutt is in here.'

Ahsoka made a face. 'Ew . . . I smell him, too!'

Anakin opened the cell door. Sitting on the cold dungeon floor was a miniature version of Jabba, no taller than Ahsoka's knee. The tiny Hutt screamed and cried.

'He's a lot younger than I thought he'd be,' Anakin remarked.

'Ah, he's just a baby. This will make our job a lot easier,' Ahsoka said. 'Besides, he's so cute!'

Anakin wasn't as charmed as Ahsoka. 'Just wait until you see what he'll grow into.'

Ahsoka ignored him and knelt down next to Rotta. The young Hutt fidgeted and cried.

Anakin talked into his comlink. 'We've got Jabba's son, Rex. Any sign of General Kenobi yet?'

'No, sir,' Rex answered.

Ahsoka tried to pick up Rotta, but the baby squirmed in her arms.

'Master, my Jedi training didn't prepare me for *this*,' she said, exasperated. 'What are we going to do?'

'Well, since you think that smelly larva is cute, you're gonna carry it,' Anakin replied.

Ahsoka opened her mouth to complain, but thought better of it. A real Jedi wouldn't back down at the simple task of carrying a baby, even if it was a slimy one. She picked up Rotta and held on tightly, trying not to let him slip through her arms.

The baby was a lot heavier than he looked. Ahsoka kept a firm grip on his slippery skin and followed Anakin out of the dungeon and up the stairs, where they picked up Rex and the clone troopers. Then they hurried through the passageway and emerged outside into the castle courtyard.

Anakin stopped, and Ahsoka was grateful for the break.

'How do you like your little buddy now? Still cute?' Anakin asked.

'No,' Ahsoka replied wearily. 'He's reminding me of you more and more.'

Anakin gave Ahsoka a stern look. Rotta saw Anakin and reached out towards him, gurgling happily.

'See? You're two of a kind,' Ahsoka said.

'Then maybe you should carry both of us,' Anakin replied.

Rotta began to cry again, and then gave a rough cough. Ahsoka balanced him in one arm and felt his forehead. The baby Hutt felt hot.

'Master, I think this little guy is sick. He's burning up with fever,' Ahsoka said.

Anakin knelt down and examined Rotta. The

baby's eyes were watery, and his tongue was slimier than it should have been.

'You're right,' Anakin said, concerned. 'We've got to get him back to the ship, immediately!'

He motioned to one of the clones. 'Trooper! Get me a backpack!'

The trooper obeyed promptly, and Anakin and Ahsoka struggled to get Rotta in the backpack. The baby squirmed and wiggled, resisting their every move.

'I hate Hutts,' Anakin grumbled.

Normally, Anakin was sensitive to any disturbance in the Force. But he was too preoccupied with Rotta to notice Asajj Ventress hidden in the shadows of the courtyard. The silver droid stood next to her, recording their every move.

Back on planet Tatooine, Count Dooku entered Jabba the Hutt's throne room. Dooku's long face was gaunt and pale under his black hooded robe. He walked up to the crime lord and bowed respectfully.

'Oh great Jabba the Hutt, I have news of your son,' he said. 'I have discovered that it is the Jedi who have kidnapped him.'

'DOOKU WANA JEEMEESHKA!' Jabba bellowed.

'How have you come by this information?'
TC-70 translated.

'I have my ways,' Dooku said. 'More importantly,
mighty Jabba, I bring a warning. The Jedi are
planning to destroy you.'

Jabba was furious. 'UHH! WOONKA MEE
CHEESKOH!'

'The most-wise Jabba demands proof,' TC-70
said.

'And he shall have it,' Count Dooku answered.
He took a holoprojector from inside his cloak, and a
hologram recording began to play. It showed Ahsoka
and Anakin cramming Rotta into the backpack as the
baby screamed and cried.

'I hate Hutts!' Anakin said.

Jabba's eyes widened in fury.

'As you can see, it is the Jedi who have your son
and are plotting against you,' Dooku calmly told
him.

'JEDI POODOO!' Jabba fumed.

'My droid army has already initiated a rescue,'
Count Dooku said. 'Rest assured, mighty Jabba, your
son will be saved.'

'HMM. ENIKI BARGON DOOKU, CHEECOPA
WUNGEE NAGA?' Jabba asked.

TC-70 translated. 'Mighty Jabba wishes to know what you ask in return.'

Count Dooku's thin mouth formed a snake-like smile. 'Perhaps you would consider joining our struggle against the Republic.'

Anakin's Delta-7 starfighter landed in the courtyard next to them. Artoo sat in the plug of the hull, piloting the ship. He projected a hologram of Obi-Wan before Anakin.

'Anakin, did you locate Jabba's son?' the Jedi asked.

'We have him, but it looks like the Separatists are behind his abduction,' Anakin reported. 'This smells like Count Dooku to me.'

'I think it's little Stinky you smell,' Ahsoka joked.

Obi-Wan frowned. 'I'll bet Dooku is using us to get Jabba to join the Separatists.'

'Master Kenobi, we have another problem,' Ahsoka chimed in. 'This Huttlet is very sick.'

'I'm not sure we can get him back to Tatooine

alive, Master,' Anakin added. 'This whole rescue may backfire on us. I still don't think dealing with the Hutts is a good idea.'

'Anakin, you know they control shipping routes in the Outer Rim. Jabba's cooperation is crucial to the war effort,' Obi-Wan said sternly. 'If you let anything happen to his son, our chances of a treaty with him will disappear.'

Bright flashes appeared in the sky behind the hologram of Obi-Wan.

'Master! We've got trouble!' Ahsoka shouted.

A Separatist landing ship broke through the clouds. Several squads of vulture droid fighters surrounded it. They dived into the courtyard, ready to attack.

'Defensive positions!' Rex yelled.

'I'll have to call you back, Master,' Anakin said. 'We're under attack. We could use a little help here, if you have the time.'

'I'll get there as soon as I can!' Obi-Wan promised as his hologram fizzled out. 'Protect the Hutt, Anakin!'

The swarm of vulture fighters descended on the courtyard like an army of flying insects. Each grey fighter bore the blue and white markings that boasted their allegiance to the Separatist cause. The unmanned fighters were small, but carried an impressive arsenal of blaster cannons, energy torpedo launchers and missile launchers.

The clone troopers fired up at the vulture droids, but there were too many to fight off, and they moved too quickly. One fighter targeted Anakin's starfighter with a well-aimed torpedo. Artoo popped out of the craft just before it exploded.

Anakin looked to the castle gates for a possible way to escape. But a new army of battle droids marched towards them. Anakin weighed his options, and none of them were very good. He shouted to Ahsoka and pointed at the castle.

'Get inside!' he yelled.

Ahsoka obeyed, dodging the rain of laser blasts with Rotta in her backpack. She watched the fray from the safety of the castle entryway.

An AT-TE walker stomped towards the front gates, trying to hold back the assault. But a squad of spider droids assaulted the tank, barraging it with heavy fire. The huge walker toppled over, crashing to the courtyard ground.

The army of droids flooded the courtyard.

'Fall back!' Anakin ordered the troops.

The outnumbered clones retreated into the castle, firing as they ran. Rex reached the entryway and activated the heavy metal door. Anakin was the last to retreat. He somersaulted under the door just as it closed.

Anakin panted, trying to catch his breath. 'Captain, we'll stay here until General Kenobi arrives with reinforcements.'

Ahsoka glared at him. 'Master, do you honestly think we can hold them off? We've got to find a way out of here.'

'Our mandate is to protect this Hutt, and that's what we're going to do, Ahsoka,' Anakin said sternly.

'Our mandate was to get this Hutt back to Tatooine, and time is running out,' Ahsoka reminded him.

Anakin glanced at Rotta. The baby had turned a sickly green colour. Ahsoka had a point. If they waited for Obi-Wan, Rotta might not make it back to Jabba alive. And that would be bad news for the Republic.

'I suppose you have a plan?' he asked.

'Yes. Or, I think so,' she replied. 'Artoo willing.'

The little droid beeped in reply.

'All right, Snips. I'll trust you on this one,' he said. Then he turned to Rex. 'Captain, hold them here as long as you can.'

'Will do, sir!' Rex replied.

Anakin, Ahsoka and Artoo headed deeper into the castle as quickly as they could. They had to find a way out – before the droid army found a way back in.

CHAPTER ELEVEN

Anakin, Ahsoka and Artoo entered the castle's throne room. Every Hutt palace had one, and Ahsoka knew the throne room was likely to have a computer hub. She was right.

Artoo rolled over to the hub. A tube-shaped interface extended from a port in the centre of his cylindrical body. He plugged the interface into the computer.

'If there's a way out of here, Artooie will find it,' Ahsoka said confidently.

Artoo beeped in agreement.

'Make it quick,' Anakin told the droid.

He glanced over at Ahsoka. Rotta had fallen asleep, and the Padawan was nearly doubled over by the weight of the backpack.

'Put him down and get some rest yourself,' he

told Ahsoka. 'It's been a long day for you, little one.'

'I can hold him, Master,' Ahsoka said stubbornly. 'I'm not tired.'

'Suit yourself,' Anakin replied, frustrated. A Padawan was supposed to respect her Master, not constantly argue with him. 'I don't see why you just won't listen to me.'

'I do listen to you, Master. I just don't like being treated like a youngling,' Ahsoka protested.

'You must have patience. What are you trying to prove, anyway?'

Ahsoka looked down at her boots. 'That I'm not too young to be your Padawan.'

Anakin put a hand on her shoulder. 'Ahsoka, a very wise Jedi once said that nothing happens by accident. It is the will of the Force that you are at my side. I just want to keep you there in one piece.'

Anakin's words were just what she needed to hear. Ahsoka was still worried that Anakin would send her back to the Jedi Temple. But he truly had her best interests at heart. She gently unstrapped the backpack and put Rotta on the ground.

Just as she put him down the sound of an explosion echoed through the castle.

'That sounded bad,' Anakin said. The battle droids had most likely blasted their way into the castle. They didn't have much time.

Fortunately, Artoo had found something useful. He beeped excitedly and then projected a hologram in front of Anakin and Ahsoka. The hologram showed the outside of the castle and the mesa. Behind the castle, on the side of the mesa, was a landing platform.

'A backdoor landing platform!' Ahsoka said.

'We'll call for a gunship when we get there,' Anakin said. 'Lead the way, Artoo.'

Anakin looked down at the backpack. It was empty.

'Where's Stinky?' Anakin wondered.

'*You* told me to put him down!' Ahsoka cried.

'Find him!' Anakin said urgently.

They didn't have to look far. Anakin heard a happy Hutt gurgle, and bent down to see Rotta crawling under the throne dais.

'Come out of there, you grubby little slug!' Anakin said crossly. He pulled Rotta by his thick little tail and stuffed him back into the backpack. Ahsoka securely strapped it to her back.

'Let's see you get away this time,' Anakin said.

Then Rex's voice blared from Anakin's comlink.

'Anakin, come in. We've held the droids, sir,' Rex said.

Anakin raised his wrist to respond to the message, and then stopped. Something didn't feel right. There was a disturbance in the Force. He felt it strongly now.

'We've held the droids, sir,' Rex repeated.

Anakin shook his head. 'That's not like Rex.'

'What is your location?' Rex asked.

Suddenly, Anakin knew the truth.

'Ventress,' he whispered. Her dark energy was unmistakable. He'd been close to it once, too close, and he vowed never to forget it.

Ahsoka knew that name. 'Count Dooku's assassin?'

Everything was clear to Anakin now. 'She's here to kill the Hutt,' he said. Rotta would die, the Jedi would be blamed, and Dooku would have a new, powerful ally. 'Come on.'

They raced across the throne room, but when they reached the bottom of the stairs, Ventress had already arrived. She stood at the top of the staircase, backed up by a squad of battle droids and four super battle droids.

There was nowhere to run. Anakin and Ahsoka's lightsabers hummed to life. Ventress and her troops marched down the stairs. The evil grin on the assassin's face sent a chill down Ahsoka's spine, but she steadily held on to her lightsaber.

Ventress removed her two lightsabers and ignited them. Their blades glowed with blood-red light. Anakin and Ahsoka carefully backed up. The two Jedi faced the dark disciple on the centre of the throne-room floor.

'Master Skywalker, I've been so looking forward to another encounter with you,' Ventress said in a voice like ice. She nodded at Ahsoka. 'I see you've found yourself a pet.'

'Careful, she bites,' Anakin warned.

'I'm no pet,' Ahsoka said, her eyes narrowing.

'Just give me the Hutt, Skywalker,' Ventress demanded. 'I will finish you first, so you won't have to watch your silly youngling die.'

Artoo quickly rolled to the computer and plugged in. He beeped once, and then the grated floor of the throne room dropped open.

Anakin, Ahsoka, Ventress and the droids plummeted into the darkness below. One battle droid teetered on the edge of the abyss. Artoo rolled up behind it and with a bump sent it falling into the hole.

Artoo twirled around, victorious.

Beep! Beep!

CHAPTER TWELVE

They all slid down a long metal chute towards the execution pit below the Hutt's throne room. Artoo's plan was drastic, but at least it had bought them some time.

Anakin and Ahsoka landed on the floor of the pit first. It was a cavernous chamber that stretched out on all sides, and against the far wall was a very large door.

Ventress shot down the chute next, followed by her droids. She immediately charged at Anakin with her two lightsabers.

'Ahsoka, the droids!' Anakin cried.

'Right!' Ahsoka ran at the nearest droid, somersaulted with the Huttlet still in her backpack, and landed on top of the droid's head. The confused droid didn't know where to attack.

She quickly thrust her lightsaber across the droid's blaster, cutting it in two. Flipping off the droid's head, she sliced through its neck with one clean blow. Then she landed on the next droid.

Anakin knew Ahsoka could take care of herself as far as the droids were concerned. He focused his energy on Ventress. The assassin assaulted him with both blades blazing, but Anakin expertly deflected them.

'Surrender now and save yourself the humiliation,' Anakin said.

Ventress flipped backwards, steadying herself.

'I've learned much since we last met,' she said. 'Let me show you.'

Ventress locked her two lightsabers together, forming one long staff with a glowing blade at each end. She expertly twirled it and then thrust the staff at Anakin.

Anakin's mind raced to develop a strategy against the unfamiliar weapon. He deflected blow after blow, but Ventress pushed him further and further back into the chamber.

A renewed energy charged through Anakin, and he heightened his attack, gaining the advantage once more. Then he delivered a surprise kick to the centre

Jedi Master Obi-Wan Kenobi

Ahsoka Tano

Anakin Skywalker and Clone Captain Rex

Anakin leads the clones into battle

Jabba the Hutt and son

The *Twilight* blasts into hyperspace

Padmé Amidala, C-3PO and Clone Commander Fox

Jabba's palace on Tatooine

Rex to the rescue

Republic gunship

Obi-Wan leads the fight

Dooku's massive droid army

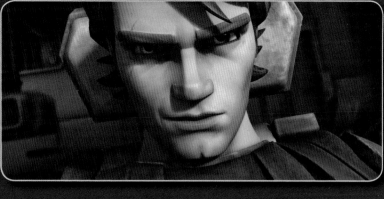

Anakin pilots the *Twilight*

Clone Commander Fox

Sith Lord Count Dooku

The Jedi battle the assassin Asajj Ventress

Padmé

Jedi Master Yoda

Clone Commander Cody gets his kicks

Rex and Obi-Wan

Anakin and Ahsoka stand their ground

Anakin and Ahsoka battle a destroyer droid

The Jedi prepare to lead the clones into battle

General Whorm Loathsom

Rex takes the lead

Ahsoka is pleased with being a Padawan

A MagnaGuard fighter explodes

Many Jedi Knights enter the fray

Supreme Chancellor Palpatine

Champions of the Republic

Asajj Ventress

General Grievous

Count Dooku

of the staff, disconnecting the two lightsabers. The weapons flew off in different directions.

But Ventress wasn't defenceless. As Anakin swung his lightsaber, she ducked and used the Force to push him backwards, taking him by surprise. He smashed against the wall, dropping his lightsaber.

Ventress held out her right hand and a lightsaber flew into it. She advanced on Anakin, pinning him against the wall.

'Prepare to join with the Force, Jedi!' she cried, igniting her weapon.

Slam! Ahsoka jumped on her back. The chamber floor behind the Padawan was littered with destroyed battle droids.

Ventress stumbled a bit. She extended her left hand and called back her other lightsaber. Then she turned, knocking Ahsoka to the ground.

Anakin quickly retrieved his lightsaber and rushed forward. He and Ahsoka locked lightsabers with Ventress. The air sizzled with energy as the three traded blows.

Slam! Ventress delivered a kick to Anakin's knees, and then spun around, slashing at Ahsoka with her blade. Ahsoka jumped back to dodge it, and Rotta fell out of the backpack.

'Stinky!' Ahsoka cried.

Anakin jumped in between Ahsoka and Ventress.

'I'll handle her!' he called out. 'Get the Huttlet out of here!'

Ahsoka picked up the heavy little Hutt. 'Easy for you to say.'

As Anakin fended off a blow from Ventress, Ahsoka raced across the chamber to the large door on the back wall. She spotted a large button on the wall and pressed it. The big door rumbled up, revealing a gigantic, clawed hand.

'Oops,' Ahsoka said. 'Not good.'

She looked up in horror to see a huge beast with long, muscled arms and a striped body. Its massive head was mostly mouth, a gaping jaw filled with teeth as sharp as knives.

Ahsoka dodged to the side as the jungle rancor stormed from its prison and attacked Ventress and Anakin, swiping at them with its claws. They jumped on to the beast's back and continued their battle. The rancor paused, puzzled. Then it noticed Ahsoka and Rotta, huddled in a corner of the chamber.

'Oh boy,' Ahsoka said nervously.

Anakin slashed the rancor's neck with his

lightsaber. The monster roared and turned away from Ahsoka, looking for its attacker.

A new squad of battle droids stormed into the throne room above them. Now they joined the fight, firing down at Anakin with their blasters. He spun around, deflecting the fire with his lightsaber. The lasers bounced back up to the throne room, striking the droids.

The rancor stomped back towards Ahsoka. She stabbed its foot with her lightsaber.

'ROOOOOOWWRR!' the beast roared. Enraged, it reared back, sending Ventress and Anakin flying off its back. They sprawled on the floor. Then the monster kicked Ahsoka, sending her skidding across the chamber. He lunged after her, and this time, she stabbed him in the nose.

Howling in pain, the rancor staggered backwards. Ventress charged at Anakin, unaware that the beast was almost upon her. The rancor collapsed on top of Ventress, and Anakin dashed away to help Ahsoka.

'Let me take that slug for a while,' he said, picking up Rotta.

'Be careful, Master,' Ahsoka warned. 'He's not well.'

'He'll be fine,' Anakin said.

Rotta gave a groan, and then hurled a spray of green vomit at Anakin. The Jedi dodged just in time.

Ahsoka laughed. 'I bet he's feeling better now.'

Anakin looked up into the throne room. 'Come on, Artoo!' he called.

Rockets sprouted from the bottom of Artoo's body. He flew down into the chamber and landed next to Anakin and Ahsoka. Then they raced for the exit.

Behind them, they heard the rancor shriek in pain.

Ventress isn't done with us yet, Anakin knew. *She won't stop until she fulfils her mission . . . and then destroys me.*

There was nothing to do but run. They followed Artoo through the maze-like halls of the castle until they reached the outdoor landing platform. Anakin activated his comlink.

'Skywalker to air support. Mark my position. I need a medical ship, immediately.'

'Acknowledged, General,' the clone pilot responded. 'I'm on my way.'

Ahsoka watched the sky, anxious for the ship to arrive.

'Ahsoka, you were a great Jedi today,' Anakin said.

'Thanks to your instruction, Master,' Ahsoka replied, pleased. Anakin's praise felt like cool water in the desert. She turned to Artoo. 'You did a swell job, too, Artooie.'

The droid chirped happily.

'You know, Skyguy, that wasn't so difficult after all,' Ahsoka said.

Anakin shook his head. 'We're not out of this yet.'

CHAPTER THIRTEEN

A Republic gunship appeared through the clouds and landed on the platform. Rotta squirmed and coughed in the pack on Anakin's back.

Ahsoka stroked his head. 'Hang in there, Stinky. We'll have you fixed up real soon.'

Anakin nodded. 'We'll get the slug here to the docs on the transport, then we're coming back for Rex.'

The clone trooper in the gunship looked anxious. 'Hurry!' he urged.

Anakin, Ahsoka and Artoo raced towards the gunship. Then a shadow passed over them. Anakin looked up to see a vulture droid bomber diving down.

'Ahsoka, wait!'

The vulture droid let loose with a barrage of

bombs, pummelling the gunship. The ship exploded in a ball of flame and light, and then toppled into the jungle below.

The blast knocked Anakin and Ahsoka off their feet and pushed Artoo on to his side. As the Jedi scrambled to recover, the vulture droid transformed into walking mode and landed on the platform, blocking their way back into the castle. The vulture droid beeped menacingly, and then opened fire.

Anakin and Ahsoka ignited their lightsabers and deflected the fierce flurry of laser blasts. Rotta started to wail loudly.

'I wish you were home, too!' Anakin cried.

Ahsoka pushed back a laserbolt with her lightsaber. 'Have you ever fought one of these things before?' she asked.

'No, but I've fought *two* of them,' Anakin joked.

The vulture droid beeped furiously, frustrated. Its weapons were not having the effect they should against these targets. It changed tactics and stomped around on the platform, trying to stab Anakin with its pointy feet. When that didn't succeed, it powered up and fired a barrage of lasers at the Jedi, forcing him back.

'Hey!' Ahsoka cried out from behind the droid, getting its attention. 'Buzz off, laser beak!'

The droid turned and opened fire on Ahsoka. She dived, rolling out of the way, losing her grip on her lightsaber. The momentum sent her rolling off the platform's edge.

'Ahsoka!' Anakin cried.

Ahsoka dangled from the platform, gripping it with her fingertips.

'Don't worry about me. I'm hanging in there, Master!' she joked.

The vulture droid hurried towards her, ready to finish her off. With a loud cry, Anakin charged, slashing at its wing. The droid turned and fired at Anakin. He gracefully deflected the blast.

Ahsoka hopped back on to the platform, held out her hand and retrieved her lightsaber. She swung hard, slicing off one of the vulture droid's legs.

The droid lost its footing, and Anakin vaulted on to its head, stabbing it between the eyes. The Jedi jumped off just as the vulture droid toppled off the platform, defeated.

'Good distraction, Snips,' Anakin panted, trying to catch his breath. 'Let me guess. You meant to do that.'

'Distraction? I cut off his leg, mortally wounding him. I don't know what you were doing,' Ahsoka said defensively.

Anakin ignored the remark and activated his wrist comlink.

'Obi-Wan, do you copy?' he asked.

Above the planet's surface, Obi-Wan and a squad of fighters were trying to come to the rescue, but a swarm of vulture droids blocked their descent.

'Anakin, do you read me? Come in,' Obi-Wan answered.

But all Anakin heard was static.

Obi-Wan frowned. 'They're jamming our transmissions. I hope Anakin is having an easier time than we are.'

Anakin lowered his wrist. 'I can't get hold of Obi-Wan. I'll see if I can find Captain Rex.'

Ahsoka ran across the platform to Artoo. The droid had been knocked backwards when the vulture droid destroyed the gunship. Ahsoka picked him up.

Beep, *beep*, Artoo chirped gratefully.

'You're welcome, Artooie,' Ahsoka said. She looked over her shoulder at Anakin. 'At least *someone* here appreciates my help.'

Anakin tried his comlink again, only to hear more static. He fiddled with the controls.

'Come in, Rex, do you copy?' he asked.

There was no reply.

'Captain Rex, respond.'

Finally he heard the clone captain's voice.

'I read you, General,' Rex replied. 'We're pinned down in the courtyard.'

'Do you need help?'

Rex didn't reply, but Anakin got his answer in a barrage of cannon fire coming from the front of the castle. It sounded like Rex and the troopers were facing a heavy assault.

'I'll take that as a yes, Captain,' Anakin said. 'Stand by. We're on our way.'

CHAPTER FOURTEEN

Anakin began to walk back into the castle. Ahsoka followed him, stunned, and Artoo trailed behind.

'Master, Stinky is really sick,' Ahsoka reminded him. 'He's turning every shade of green except the one he's supposed to be! Our mission was to get him back to Tatooine, alive.'

Anakin turned to her. 'Obi-Wan will get here eventually. Right now, we need Rex to help us find a ship.'

Ahsoka looked at Rotta, still safe in the backpack on Anakin's back. The Huttlet gave a weak cough. Reluctantly, she followed Anakin from the platform.

A familiar hum filled the air, and two destroyer droids appeared at the end of the corridor and began rolling right towards them. They shot rapid fire as they zoomed down the hall.

'Great. Rolling death balls,' Ahsoka moaned.

The Jedi activated their lightsabers and began deflecting the blasts. They backed out on to the landing platform once more. The rolling droids kept coming.

'Artoo, the door!' Anakin cried.

Artoo quickly rolled to the door control. Behind the rolling droids, Anakin could see another danger: Ventress with her lightsabers glowing brightly.

Whoosh! The metal door shut just in time. Anakin sighed with relief. Then he felt a surge of heat from the other side of the door. Ventress was cutting a hole into the metal with her lightsabers.

'I think now's a good time for a retreat,' Anakin suggested.

'Retreat? That's a new word for you,' Ahsoka said.

Anakin walked to the end of the platform. 'Maybe head into the jungle.' He looked over the edge to see several spider droids climbing up the rock wall. They fired at the bottom of the platform, rocking it. A swarm of giant dragonflies perched underneath flew up into the air, scattering. Anakin jumped back from the edge.

'So much for going that way,' he said.

He glanced back at the door. Ventress was halfway through. Suddenly, the platform shuddered under their feet.

Anakin frowned. 'Looks like we're out of options.'

Ahsoka scanned their surroundings, looking for some kind of escape. From his perch in the backpack, Rotta began to point and squeal.

'Not now, Stinky!'

But the little Hutt began to squirm with excitement. He pointed to something sparkling in the distance. It was another mesa, topped with a landing platform and a ship!

'Master, look!' Ahsoka cried.

Anakin turned and saw the ship, pleased. 'Just what we need.'

'Nice work, Stinky,' Ahsoka told Rotta. But there was one problem. 'How are we going to get over there?'

Anakin's blue eyes shone with excitement. 'Leave that to me!'

He broke into a run, and jumped right off the platform! Ahsoka gasped.

Then Anakin appeared once more, hanging on to the back of a giant dragonfly. He struggled to get control of the insect.

Ahsoka looked at Artoo, amazed. 'I hope I don't have to learn to do that.'

Artoo beeped in agreement.

Bam! Ventress burst through the doorway, lightsabers blazing. She lunged at Ahsoka, striking first with one blade, then another.

Whoosh! Whoosh! Whoosh! The hum of burning energy filled the air as Ahsoka bravely deflected the blows. But the assassin was too powerful for the young Padawan to overcome. Ventress kicked her, knocking her to the ground. She leaned over Ahsoka, ready to deliver one final strike.

'Where is Skywalker?' she hissed.

'Right here, Ventress!' Anakin called out. He flew the dragonfly into her, knocking her backwards. Ahsoka jumped to her feet.

Beneath them, the spider droids barraged the platform with another attack. The floor began to break underneath them.

Ventress jumped up and somersaulted backwards, landing safely inside the doorway just as the platform fell. Ahsoka's stomach lurched as she felt the platform plunge beneath her.

'Hold on, Snips!' Anakin called out.

'Like I have a choice!' Ahsoka cried, stretching

out her hand. Anakin grabbed it just in time, pulling her on to the dragonfly with him.

Artoo activated his rockets and flew beside them. Below, the pieces of the broken platform fell to the jungle floor. Ahsoka tightened her grip on Anakin, pressing herself against Rotta, who was still strapped to the Jedi's back. The baby belched unhappily in her face.

'Yuck!' Ahsoka grimaced. 'Yeah, I missed you, too.'

They flew towards the other mesa, where the ship waited for them. Anakin hoped the craft could fly.

Unless Obi-Wan flew out of the sky to rescue them, that ship was their only hope.

CHAPTER FIFTEEN

Vulture droid fighters raced through the airspace above Teth, attacking Obi-Wan Kenobi and his fleet like a swarm of angry bees. Obi-Wan released fire from both the front and rear cannons, blasting two vulture droids out of the sky.

Up ahead, four of the small enemy fighters surrounded one of the clone gunships. The clone pilot, Oddball, frantically called out over the comm system.

'I'm hit! I can't shake 'em!'

'Just relax, Oddball,' Obi-Wan reassured him. 'I'm right behind you.'

Obi-Wan streaked into the fray, circling the fighters and taking them out one by one. They spiralled through the sky, exploding in mid-air.

'Thank you, sir,' Oddball said. 'Sorry I panicked.'

'That's all right. It happens to everybody,' Obi-Wan told him.

He dipped down over the planet and surveyed the situation. Most of the vulture droids had been destroyed in the skirmish. But clouds of smoke from cannon blasts rose up from the castle.

'It looks like there's some kind of battle on the east side of the palace,' Obi-Wan reported over the comm system.

'I see it, sir,' Commander Cody replied. He was stationed in the Jedi cruiser in front of another fleet of gunships.

'And if there's a battle, Anakin's probably in the middle of it,' Obi-Wan reasoned. 'We'll start looking for him there. All ships follow me. Commander Cody, prepare the gunships for ground assault.'

But Anakin was nowhere near the castle. He and Ahsoka flew to the landing pad and jumped off the dragonfly. Artoo touched down beside them.

The ship that had glittered so magnificently from the distance was an old, beat-up freighter. The faded paint on the side announced its name: *Twilight*.

'We're taking this junker?' Ahsoka asked, unbelieving. 'We'd be better off on that big bug.'

'Get on board and prime the engines,' Anakin

said, ignoring her remark. *Assuming it has engines*, he thought, keeping his concerns to himself. The *Twilight* was all they had; there was no use complaining about it.

Ahsoka walked to the entry ramp and pressed a button. The ramp lowered, and to Ahsoka's surprise, she saw the silver droid from the castle standing there.

'Hey, you're that caretaker droid,' she said. 'I wondered what happened to you.'

The droid seemed startled. 'Oh, uh, young one . . . I mean, soon to be Jedi Knight. Uh, I had to get away from the terrible trouble at . . .'

A battle droid walked down the ramp, interrupting him. 'Okay, everything loaded. Let's get out of here.'

Then the battle droid noticed Ahsoka. She scowled at the caretaker droid.

'Why, you tin-plated traitor!'

The spydroid's silver eyes gleamed. 'Blast her!' he commanded.

More battle droids charged down the ramp, firing at Ahsoka. She ran towards them, her lightsaber blazing green.

Slash! Slice! Slash! She cut down their weapons

before delivering a final blow to each surprised battle droid. Their smoking metal bodies littered the entry ramp. She faced the spydroid, angry.

'Don't you dare!' the droid protested.

Whoosh! Ahsoka sliced off the spydroid's head with one blow. His head rolled to the bottom of the ramp and landed at Anakin's feet. The Jedi smiled. He carried Rotta up the ramp, and he, Ahsoka and Artoo entered the now-safe ship.

In the castle courtyard, Rex's forces were locked in a furious shoot-out with the droid troops. The clones put up a good fight, but there were just too many battle droids and super battle droids. The droids cut down clone after clone, forming a circle around Rex and his men. The battle droid captain stepped forward.

'Surrender, Republic dogs!' he yelled.

CHAPTER SIXTEEN

Rex would not give up easily.

'We've got you outnumbered!' he shot back.

This confused the droid captain, just as Rex knew it would. 'Outnumbered? Wait. One . . . two . . .'

BAM! The battle droid and the droids surrounding him exploded in a fiery blast. A scream of engines drowned out the droids' alarmed cries as a Jedi interceptor dived over the castle. The sleek craft had a pair of dagger-like wings and a ball-shaped, single-man cockpit in the centre. The cockpit door popped open and Obi-Wan jumped out, somersaulting into the courtyard, slashing droids as he landed. His astromech, R4-P17, flew off in the interceptor.

Now a squad of Republic gunships swooped down, cannons blazing. They fired on the droids, toppling them.

Obi-Wan fought from the ground. He Force-pushed one advancing droid against the castle wall, and then turned to slash two more droids with his lightsaber.

Commander Cody joined the ground battle, leading a fresh squad of clone troops into the courtyard. Rex was relieved to see reinforcements arrive at last.

Obi-Wan ran up to Rex. They stood side by side, fending off battle droids.

'Where's Skywalker?' Obi-Wan asked.

'Best guess says he's still in the castle, sir,' Rex replied.

'Keep the droids occupied,' Obi-Wan instructed. 'I'll go find him!'

Inside the castle's entry corridor, a squad of super battle droids surrounded Ventress. She talked to Count Dooku on a holoprojector.

'Have you recovered Jabba's son?' Dooku asked.

A dark cloud crossed Ventress's face. 'Skywalker is still in possession of the Hutt and has temporarily eluded me, but he will not escape the system alive.'

Count Dooku did not look pleased. 'Need I remind you that whoever gains Jabba's favour will control the war in the Outer Rim?' he said crossly.

'Only *we* must be allowed to return Jabba's son to him, alive.'

'I understand, Master. I will double my efforts.'

'I hope so, for your sake,' he said ominously. Then the hologram faded.

Angry now, Ventress activated her lightsabers. She turned to see a bearded Jedi standing in the doorway. She sneered.

'Master Kenobi. Always chasing after Skywalker. How predictable.'

Obi-Wan steeled himself at the sight of the assassin. He had faced her before, and although she had never been formally trained as a Sith, her command of the dark side of the Force was strong.

'Anakin leaves quite a mess,' he replied. 'Which always leads me to you, Ventress.'

'Take him!' Ventress ordered the super battle droids.

She ran for a side exit. Anakin Skywalker was a powerful Jedi, but she knew Obi-Wan was even stronger.

The sharp scent of sizzling energy filled the air as Obi-Wan delivered a blow to the head of her droid escort. The droid fell to the floor, circuits sparking. Obi-Wan stepped over the fallen droid and chased after Ventress.

The door she had stepped through led to a dark room containing rows of tall columns. He stepped inside carefully, knowing that she could be hiding behind any one of them.

'Ventress, I know you're here,' he called out. 'You can't hide. I feel your frustration. Let me guess: you're after Jabba's son, too.'

'HA!'

Ventress exploded out of the blackness, striking at Obi-Wan with her twin swords.

Obi-Wan parried, thrusting his lightsaber twice as fast to keep up with the double barrage of blows. Ventress spun around, throwing her cloak at him. He stepped aside, missing it.

'You'll have to do better than that, my darling,' he said.

Ventress growled, charging at Obi-Wan. She fought fiercely, twirling around the Jedi like a desert wind. He moved quickly to keep up with her, but she delivered one quick, unexpected thrust to the handle of his lightsaber. It clattered to the castle floor.

'Well, now I'm impressed,' Obi-Wan quipped.

Ventress lunged forward, prepared to kill the unarmed Jedi.

'Now you die!'

CHAPTER SEVENTEEN

Anakin, Ahsoka and Artoo stepped inside the *Twilight*. The old freighter was a mess of grimy control panels and exposed wiring. Ahsoka sat in the co-pilot's chair, Rotta in her lap. Anakin located the button to start the engines.

'Now, let's get Stinky out of here,' he said, trying to sound confident. He pressed the button and nothing happened. 'Uh, if we can.'

Ahsoka groaned.

'Relax, Snips,' Anakin told her. 'Artoo, see if you can spark the ignition couplers.'

Whistle, beep! Artoo plugged into a nearby console. He beeped a go-ahead to Anakin. The Jedi tried to start the engines again, but they still wouldn't fire.

Anakin frowned. 'That's not it. Try opening the fuel lifters all the way.'

Artoo's interface spun around, and in a few seconds, the engines began to rumble. The baby Hutt squealed happily in Ahsoka's lap.

Anakin grinned. 'Good work, buddy!'

The *Twilight* lifted off the landing pad and rocketed towards the castle. Ahsoka looked out of the window and saw the gunships in Obi-Wan's fleet battling the droids in the courtyard.

'Master Kenobi is here!' she cried. 'Now we'll see some real fireworks.'

'Excuse me?' Anakin asked, offended. 'What do you call what I've been doing all day?'

'I don't know. The word "reckless" comes to mind,' Ahsoka replied.

'Very funny, Snips,' Anakin said. He studied the control panel in front of him. 'Back to work. The troops still need our help. Charge the main guns.'

Rotta the Hutt gave a sickly cough. Ahsoka felt the baby's head. It was burning hot.

'How are we going to help?' she asked. 'Stinky's getting sicker and sicker.'

Anakin was torn about what to do. 'We promised Rex we'd help him.'

'Master, we've got to get Stinky to the medics on the Jedi cruiser,' Ahsoka said seriously. 'It's our only chance to get him back to his father, still breathing.'

Anakin knew his Padawan was right. He reluctantly activated the comlink.

'Captain Rex, this is General Skywalker.'

'Yes, General,' Rex replied.

'We're not going to be able to help you,' Anakin told him. It pained him to say it. He could hear the sounds of heavy combat in the background.

'Don't worry about us, General,' Rex said. 'We'll be all right.'

Anakin piloted the freighter away from the castle and headed for the clouds. It wouldn't take long to reach the Jedi cruiser, where they could get help for Stinky and get a proper ship to take to Tatooine. A hopeful quiet came over the cockpit.

The Jedi were silent for a moment. Then Ahsoka spoke up.

'Master, I did my best to stay calm and focused today,' she said. 'And when I did, everything seemed so easy.'

Before Anakin could respond, the ship broke through a bank of clouds . . . and emerged into a fierce battle! The Jedi cruiser and a Separatist battleship were exchanging fire. The cruiser was a long, sleek ship with rear wings and a body shaped like the nose of a shark. The large Separatist warship was an imposing sight: it was disc-shaped, with a large central sphere. Republic V-19 starfighters and vulture droids buzzed wildly between the larger ships.

'Well, things just got a lot harder,' Anakin remarked.

Three of the vulture droid fighters spotted the *Twilight*. They veered around and zoomed towards the freighter.

'All we've got to do is land on that Jedi cruiser,' Anakin said, trying to stay focused.

'But, Master, the cruiser's deflector shields are up!' Ahsoka realized. The cruiser would have to lower its shields to allow them to land, and risk taking damage from the battleship.

The dark sky lit up with orange fire as the two big ships pummelled each other with cannon blasts. Anakin expertly piloted the ship between the explosions, trying to avoid the pursuing vulture droids at the same time.

The Jedi cruiser was almost in reach.

Bam! The cruiser fired at the *Twilight*. The small ship rocked from the impact. Ahsoka held on to Rotta, trying to keep them both steady.

'They must think this grease bucket is an enemy ship,' Ahsoka realized.

Anakin scrambled to activate the comlink. 'Jedi cruiser, hold your fire!'

The voice of a clone officer replied over the comlink. 'Who is that? Incoming ship, identify yourself!'

'This is General Skywalker,' Anakin answered. 'We have Jabba the Hutt's son. He needs medical attention. We must board immediately.'

'Stand by.'

'Stand by? That's helpful,' Ahsoka grumbled.

Boom! Now the freighter took a hit from behind, as one of the vulture droids' cannons targeted it.

'Hold on!' Anakin shouted.

He flew the freighter clear over the top of the Jedi cruiser. Then he flipped the ship upside down. Ahsoka held on to Rotta tightly, trying not to fall. Artoo slid across the floor. The vulture droids chased them all the way around the cruiser.

There was a hiss of static from the comlink.

'General Skywalker, we think we can lift the shields on the lower rear hangar,' the clone officer informed them.

'We're on our way,' Anakin said.

He made a sharp turnaround, losing the vulture droids for a few seconds. Then he pushed the freighter as fast as it would go, speeding towards the back of the cruiser. The doors opened, and the blue light of the shields fizzled out.

'We've made it. We've made it!' Ahsoka cried.

The *Twilight* dived down into the hangar, ready to land, when . . .

BOOM! The hangar exploded in a deafening blast of white light.

The clone officer's panicked voice came over the comlink.

'You can't land! You can't land!'

Anakin pulled back hard on the thrusters, and the *Twilight* quickly pulled up and away from the cruiser. The vulture droids flew right behind them, getting closer with each second.

'That changes our plans,' Anakin said. Ahsoka couldn't believe how calm he sounded. 'Looks like we're going to have to take this bucket of bolts all the way to Tatooine.'

Anakin pulled back on the thrusters again, but the ship could not go any faster. White-hot blasts of fire from the pursuing droids streaked past the windows.

'We'll never outrun those droids with this weight,'

Anakin said. 'We've got to ditch whatever's in the cargo bay. Open the rear doors.'

'Got it,' Ahsoka said, eager to do something useful. 'Prepare to be impressed.'

She plopped Rotta in a chair and quickly rushed out of the cockpit.

'Ahsoka, wait!' Anakin called after her, but the Padawan didn't hear him.

She opened the door to the cargo bay to see it filled with crates.

'Losing this ought to lighten us up,' Ahsoka reasoned. She located the room's control panel, and hit the button controlling the rear door. It opened with a hiss.

'Master, the cargo doors are open,' Ahsoka reported into the comlink.

In the cockpit, Anakin pulled back on the controls. The *Twilight* began to climb, going straight up. The vulture droids followed it, staying close behind.

Then, abruptly, the ship tilted sharply, pointing up. The heavy crates began to tumble out of the open cargo door, and Ahsoka began to fall towards the open door. She reached out and grabbed a dangling air hose.

'I knew we shouldn't have taken this worthless grease bucket,' she complained. She strained to hold on as her hands began to lose their grip.

Behind her, the crates all plummeted out of the ship. From the cockpit, Anakin saw the falling crates crash right into the pursuing vulture droids. The enemy ships exploded from the impact.

Anakin smiled. 'That's better.'

He looked behind him, expecting to see that Ahsoka had returned. But she wasn't there.

'Ahsoka, where are you? Time to get out of here!'

Ahsoka wanted nothing more than to leave that cargo hold. But if she let go of the hose, she'd go flying out into space through the open door.

Calm and focused, she remembered. She closed her eyes, trying to clear her mind. There had to be some way to close that door . . .

She opened her eyes. She had it! She held on tightly with one hand and freed her lightsaber with the other. Then she took a deep breath and hurled it at the control panel. The metal handle slammed into the button, and the door slid shut.

Ahsoka hopped on to the floor. She affectionately patted the hull of the ship.

'Grease bucket, forgive me,' she said. 'You're my favourite ship ever.'

Breathless, she made her way back to the cockpit and plopped down into the co-pilot's chair. Rotta was fussing and squealing. She stroked the little Hutt's head, and the baby calmed down.

'It wasn't easy, but I found a way,' she said.

'Yeah, the long way,' Anakin informed her. 'The cargo door control is right under your nose.'

He nodded towards the co-pilot's control panel. The button for the cargo door was clearly marked. She could have released the crates without even leaving her seat. She frowned.

Anakin turned to Artoo. 'We're clear to make the jump to hyperspace. Artoo, program the navi-computer.'

Artoo plugged in his interface and got to work. Next to Ahsoka, Rotta coughed hoarsely.

'I don't think we're going to make it, Master,' Ahsoka said worriedly. 'There's got to be something we can do for him.'

'Take a look in the back,' Anakin suggested. 'See if you can find some medical supplies.'

Ahsoka rushed out of the cockpit once more. 'I'm on it.'

Rotta gasped weakly and looked up at Anakin.

'Don't die on me, little guy,' Anakin told him. 'Just hang in there.'

Artoo beeped at Anakin. They were ready to leave.

'If you've locked the coordinates, Artoo, let's go,' Anakin said.

Artoo turned his interface. The ship lurched.

The *Twilight* jumped into hyperspace, headed for Tatooine.

CHAPTER EIGHTEEN

Back on Teth, Ventress swung both her lightsabers at
Obi-Wan Kenobi. The Jedi reached up and grabbed
her hands, stopping the attack. Now the two were
face-to-face.

'Hello,' Obi-Wan said cheerfully.

Ventress pulled herself from his grasp. The Jedi
Force-pushed the assassin away from him and sent
her flying into a nearby column. He extended his
hand and his lightsaber leaped into it. He smiled as
she jumped to her feet, spinning around to face him.

'Shall we continue?' Obi-Wan asked.

'My pleasure,' Ventress said, her dark eyes
narrowed.

She rushed forward, thrusting one lightsaber at
him. He deflected the attack with his own glowing
blue blade.

Then Obi-Wan took the offensive, lunging forward with one swift blow after another. Ventress deflected each one with skill.

Perhaps a change of venue, Obi-Wan thought. He jumped up, landing on top of one of the columns. Ventress propelled herself up and landed on another column, facing him.

'We know of Dooku's plot to turn the Hutts against us,' Obi-Wan informed her. 'It will not succeed.'

'It will when the truth dies with you,' Ventress said angrily. She lunged towards him with unrestrained fury, thrusting her twin lightsabers at the same time. Obi-Wan jumped backwards down the row of columns, until he reached an open window. With a grin, he jumped outside.

Ventress scowled. 'You can't run!' she cried. She jumped out of the window after him.

Obi-Wan balanced on one of the castle's narrow stone walls. He aimed a blow at Ventress as she jumped on to the wall next to him. She smoothly deflected it, then crouched, ready to strike.

Suddenly, she glanced skyward. Obi-Wan felt a ripple in the Force at the same time. He grinned knowingly.

'I sense it, too,' he said. 'Anakin is gone. You've failed, Ventress.'

He jumped up, swinging his lightsaber before she could prepare herself for the attack. The Jedi knocked one of the lightsabers out of Ventress's hand.

'Your Master will not be pleased,' Obi-Wan reminded her. Not even an assassin as tough as Ventress wanted to face Count Dooku's rage.

Ventress pressed a button on a metal band on her wrist. She glared at Obi-Wan.

'Jedi scum!' She spat out the words.

'The Hutt is safe. There's no point in fighting any longer,' Obi-Wan said calmly. 'We've won. Lay down your weapon.'

Suddenly, a vulture droid fighter swooped down from the sky. Ventress jumped on to the fighter as it raced past.

Obi-Wan watched with unease as the ship flew off. Jabba's son was safe with Anakin now, but he would have preferred it if Ventress were not on the loose.

Would the assassin give up so easily?

The *Twilight* rocketed through the swirling hyperspace tunnel. To Anakin's relief, the old ship somehow stayed steady when hit with the rigours of interdimensional space travel.

Rotta slept on a bunk in the cockpit, snoring contentedly. Then he opened his eyes, looked at Ahsoka and Anakin, and smiled.

'Master, the medicine is working!' Ahsoka said, relieved. She felt his forehead. 'His fever broke. I think he's gonna live to stink another day.'

She gently caressed his head, and the baby Hutt snuggled deeper into the bunk. Across the cockpit, Anakin and Artoo were working on repairing the ship.

'Great,' Anakin said, looking up from the console. 'Keeping him alive wasn't as easy as you'd hoped, was it?'

'Master, if you've taught me one thing, it's that nothing is easy when you're around,' Ahsoka said. She started to laugh, but Anakin raised a warning eyebrow, so she changed the subject. 'You think Rex and Obi-Wan made out okay?'

'If I know my old Master, he has things well in hand,' Anakin assured her. 'Now help me with this. I want the primary systems repaired by the time we reach Tatooine.'

Ahsoka left Rotta and joined Anakin.

'You grew up on Tatooine, right?' Ahsoka asked. 'So for you, this trip is like going home.'

Anakin narrowed his eyes. A flood of bitter memories welled up inside him, but he pushed them down. He wasn't exactly anxious to return to Tatooine. But at least Rotta was safe. They could touch down, drop off the Huttlet, and then leave Tatooine as quickly as they could.

That was Anakin's plan, but Ventress had other ideas. She may have failed her mission, but she was not ready to give up. She flew the vulture droid back to the castle, and contacted Count Dooku on a holoprojector. Dooku received the message in Jabba's throne room.

'The Republic had too many clone troopers, my lord,' she said, her eyes lowered. 'By the time we were able to find Jabba's son, Skywalker had already killed him.'

Jabba let out a bellow of pain and fury.

'Most unfortunate,' Count Dooku said smoothly. 'This is a very unexpected turn of events. I take it you at least defeated the Jedi?'

'No, Master. The Jedi escaped and are headed to Tatooine,' Ventress reported.

Count Dooku clenched his teeth as he realized the truth. Ventress had failed, and now Skywalker was headed here with Jabba's son.

'I'm sure you did the best you could,' he replied. 'We will discuss your failure later.'

'Yes, my Master.' Ventress bowed, and the hologram disappeared.

Jabba's angry voice shook the throne room. 'AH! YAPOTA JEDI AMA TATOOINE?'

'Glorious Jabba demands to know why the Jedi would dare to come to Tatooine,' TC-70 asked.

'To kill *you*, Jabba,' Count Dooku lied. 'The Jedi plot is quite clear now. They only promised to rescue your son to win your trust. Now Skywalker is coming here to finish his true mission, to wipe out the entire Hutt clan.'

'JEDI SLEEMO!' Jabba howled.

'If it pleases you, mighty Jabba, this time I will deal with Skywalker personally,' Count Dooku suggested.

A crowd of deadly looking MagnaGuard droids appeared behind Dooku. Red eyes glowed spookily on their blank metal faces. Each MagnaGuard droid carried a long staff that sizzled with electric energy in attack mode.

Jabba nodded, pleased. This would be a fitting end to a treacherous Jedi like Skywalker.

Dooku bowed to Jabba, turned away and finally allowed himself to smile.

Ventress may have failed, but he would not. He would intercept the Jedi, kill the young Hutt, and destroy Skywalker once and for all.

CHAPTER NINETEEN

The *Twilight* sailed out of hyperspace. The ship emerged from the tunnel into calm, open space. The planet Tatooine glowed orange below them. Anakin and Artoo were working on the ship's engineering console, trying to ready the ship for a safe landing.

Ahsoka sat in the co-pilot's seat, gazing down at the planet. Anakin had been all over the galaxy, but Ahsoka's journey as a Jedi was just beginning. Each new place she saw fascinated her.

'Welcome home, Skyguy,' Ahsoka said happily. 'I bet it feels great to be back.' She hadn't been on her own home planet in a long time. She'd be glad to see it again.

But Anakin wasn't happy at all. 'I was hoping I'd never have to lay eyes on this dust ball again.'

'Okay . . . what happened?' Ahsoka ventured.

'I don't want to talk about it,' Anakin said, avoiding her eyes. 'How's Stinky holding up?'

Ahsoka leaned back to the cot where Rotta was sleeping. The little Hutt's eyes were closed, his breathing was normal, and his skin was cool.

'He seems to be feeling much better,' Ahsoka reported. 'His fever is gone. Even *you* have to admit that he's cute when he's asleep.'

'I admit I like him better when he's quiet, but only a little,' Anakin said, smiling slightly. He turned back to the open panel. Artoo beeped.

'No, Artoo. I want the cannon operational first. Leave the rear deflector shields for later,' Anakin instructed.

'No rear shields, Master?' Ahsoka asked. 'That's awfully risky.'

'A strong attack eliminates the need for defence, Snips,' Anakin told her. If they faced any trouble when the ship landed, they'd need their cannons to work.

Suddenly, the wail of a warning siren filled the cockpit, and lights on the control panel blinked furiously. Ahsoka checked the ship's scanner, but the screen was fuzzy. She banged on it, and an image of two MagnaGuard fighter ships appeared.

'Attack ships closing!' Ahsoka cried.

'Set the approach vector and get ready to land,' Anakin instructed her.

Ahsoka reached for the controls just as the ship rocked, hit by a MagnaGuard fighter's cannons.

'Somebody doesn't want Stinky to get home in one piece,' Anakin realized.

The freighter took another barrage of fire from the fighters, and the cockpit shook violently.

'Wow. Quite a welcome-home party,' Ahsoka joked, hanging on to the console.

'Ahsoka, activate the guns!' Anakin ordered.

Ahsoka flipped a switch in front of her and a row of green lights lit up on the control panel.

'All the guns are locked in the forward position,' she informed him. 'It's too bad you decided not to repair the rear deflector shields.'

'Not now, Ahsoka!' Anakin scolded. He worked quickly, trying to finish reworking the engineering panel. 'Artoo, see if you can unlock those guns!'

'Sometimes a good defence is the best offence,' Ahsoka muttered.

Anakin shot her a stern look. 'Why don't you go secure your little Huttlet friend?'

Ahsoka reluctantly obeyed. 'None of us are

secure with you flying,' she grumbled under her
breath.

Another blast hit the ship, and Anakin rushed to
the pilot's chair.

'Hang on back there!' he warned.

He pulled down on the controls, and the *Twilight*
banked sharply, swinging around to face the
attacking MagnaGuard fighters. Rotta fell out of the
bunk, and Ahsoka dived and caught him just before
he hit the floor. The Huttlet's eyes popped open and
he began to cry.

'Great! You woke the baby!' Ahsoka
complained.

'I'm a little busy here!' Anakin called back.

He flew the ship right at the MagnaGuard
fighters, letting loose a blast from the ship's cannons.

Boom! The laser blast made a direct hit,
destroying one of the Magna fighters.

'Got one of them!' Anakin cheered.

But Ahsoka wasn't ready to celebrate. 'What
about the other one?'

'One thing at a time,' Anakin barked back.

The second MagnaGuard fighter circled around to
attack the ship from behind. The ship's interior lights
blinked on and off as another blast exploded into the

freighter's rear. Through the window, Anakin could see a piece of the rear hull break off, exploding into pieces.

The ship gave a sickening creak.

'I think we needed those rear shields after all,' Anakin admitted.

The off-balance ship tilted sharply, and Ahsoka slid across the floor.

'I told you sooooooo!'

'Artoo! Turn those guns around!' Anakin ordered.

Artoo beeped and extended his interface to plug into the computer, but the ship rocked again, sending Artoo rolling away.

Beep, beep, beep!

'Artoo!' Anakin cried.

Still carrying Rotta, Ahsoka leaped in front of Artoo, pushing him back to the console with her feet. She could barely steady the heavy droid.

'Why can't you be a tiny little mouse droid?' she complained, grunting.

Artoo buzzed at her, insulted. He plugged back into the console and got to work.

Bam! The ship took another hit.

Beep, beep! Artoo's interface spun wildly. The

ship's cannon pivoted, aiming at the remaining fighter. Artoo chirped, happy, as he got ready to fire.

'Get him, Artoo!' Anakin urged.

Artoo shot the cannon, and the MagnaGuard swiftly dodged it. The enemy ship turned back around and returned fire on the freighter, blasting the rear of the ship.

Artoo locked the cannon on the fighter and aimed another attack.

Boom! The MagnaGuard fighter exploded in flames.

'Good shot, buddy!' Anakin said, impressed. 'You've been holding out on me.'

Beep, beep! Artoo replied, pleased. His dish antennas popped out of the dome on top of his head and gave a victory spin.

The MagnaGuard fighters might have been taken care of, but the ship still had to land. Anakin knew that wasn't going to be easy without a rear hull.

Anakin turned to Ahsoka. 'Strap in.'

She sat in the chair and obeyed. 'You've got that "we're in trouble" look.'

'There's a look?'

'You can't miss it,' Ahsoka assured him.

'Very funny, Snips,' Anakin replied. He flipped on his dash communicator.

'Obi-Wan, come in! Do you copy?'

'Kenobi here,' Obi-Wan replied. 'Anakin, have you reached Tatooine yet?'

Bam! The ship rocked from another blast. More enemy fighters had joined the fight.

'Almost, but we ran into some old . . .' Anakin hesitated to tell his old Master the truth.

'Anakin, did you get shot down again?' Obi-Wan asked.

'YES!' Ahsoka shouted.

Anakin shot her a dirty look.

'This ship is too slow,' Anakin tried to explain. 'I haven't had time to modify it yet.'

'I'm still cleaning up your other mess, but I'll get there,' Obi-Wan promised.

Anakin shook his head. 'So much for reinforcements.'

The ship sped towards the planet's surface, cutting a blazing path through the atmosphere. As the sandy surface of Tatooine came into view, the ship shuddered.

'Hang on,' Anakin warned. 'This landing could get a little rough.'

'Crashes are rough,' Ahsoka pointed out. 'Landings are not.'

'Then it's a crash landing.'

The entire hull of the ship flamed as it hurtled through the atmosphere. The *Twilight* touched down, skimming over the sand. Ahsoka held on to Rotta as tightly as she could. Through the window, she could see small creatures in brown hooded robes fleeing as they sped past. Clouds of sand whipped up against the ship.

The freighter gradually slowed, then slammed into a sand dune, finally grinding to a stop.

For better or worse, they had landed on Tatooine.

CHAPTER TWENTY

On planet Coruscant, Yoda met with Chancellor Palpatine in the Senate leader's office. They watched a hologram of Obi-Wan projected above Palpatine's desk.

'Anakin reached Tatooine with the Huttlet, Master,' Obi-Wan reported. 'But he's still in grave danger. Separatist troops are desperate to intercept him. I think this whole plot was engineered by Dooku to convince Jabba we kidnapped his son.'

'If believe this the Hutts do, ended our chance of a treaty with them will be,' Yoda said gravely. 'Join Dooku and the Separatists Jabba will. Yes.'

'That would be a disaster,' Chancellor Palpatine said. The white-haired man looked dignified in his brown senatorial robes. 'We *must* have this allegiance with the Hutts if we are to win the war in the Outer Rim.'

Yoda nodded. 'In Skywalker is the Republic's only hope. Return Jabba's son, he must.'

Obi-Wan was confident. 'Anakin's experience with the Hutts should help. He'll come through!'

The hologram of Obi-Wan faded just as Padmé Amidala appeared in the chancellor's doorway. The former Queen of Naboo was now a respected Galactic Senator. She was dressed in a simple purple robe with a green collar, a garment befitting of a senator. Her brown hair was piled high on top of her head, and a silver headpiece decorated her forehead.

Palpatine noticed her and smiled. Senator Amidala was an old ally and it was with her help that he had taken the seat of chancellor.

'Excuse me, Master Yoda, I must return to the grand adventure of politics,' Palpatine told the Jedi.

Yoda hopped out of his seat and nodded in greeting as he approached Padmé.

'Master Yoda, so good to see you,' Padmé said warmly.

'Good it is to see you, Senator,' Yoda replied.

Padmé bowed respectfully, and the Jedi Master left the room. She turned to Palpatine.

'Ah, Padmé,' he began. 'We were to discuss . . .'

'The new security measures you put into Naboo,'

Padmé said, concerned. 'My security chief tells me there are several new battles in the Outer Rim.'

'Including a small skirmish with Obi-Wan Kenobi and Anakin,' the chancellor informed her.

Padmé's heart skipped a beat. 'Anakin! Is he in danger?'

Palpatine leaned across the desk. The look on his face told he was about to reveal a secret.

'I'm afraid the Jedi's efforts to strike a secret treaty with the Hutts has gone horribly wrong,' Palpatine told her. 'Jabba believes Anakin has abducted his infant son.'

'A Jedi would never do such a thing!' Padmé cried. 'Perhaps I can get that treaty signed. I will go to the Hutts and convince them of Anakin's innocence . . . as a representative of the Senate, of course.'

'That is very courageous of you, Senator, but far too dangerous,' Palpatine cautioned. 'Besides, we've attempted to contact Jabba. He won't accept communication from us.'

'Jabba the Hutt has an uncle in the old downtown area here in Coruscant,' Padmé said. 'Perhaps I can reason with him and reopen negotiations.'

Palpatine looked concerned. 'Please, my dear, I beg you, reconsider this.'

'Don't worry, Chancellor,' Padmé replied. 'I've dealt with far worse than the Hutts.'

She turned towards the door. Palpatine called out to her.

'Do take care, Senator . . . the Hutts are vile gangsters!'

Padmé stormed down the halls of the senate building. Anakin would never kidnap a baby! How dare the Hutts accuse him of such a thing.

Stay calm, she advised herself. *Your true feelings must not show.*

Padmé and Anakin were in love, but it was bittersweet. As a Galactic Senator, Padmé was expected to marry someone in her own class, and, as a Jedi, Anakin was not supposed to marry at all. But they had defied what was expected of them, and married in a secret ceremony months before. Her heart ached every time Anakin left to fight a new battle somewhere in the galaxy. And now his life might be in danger. She couldn't sit by and do nothing.

Palpatine was right. The Hutts were dangerous. She went to her quarters and changed into a more practical outfit: a simple, white hooded cloak worn over a white bodysuit. It was a lot easier to run from an angry Hutt in that than in a flowing Senator's robe.

She took a transport to the Hutt palace that towered over the streets of old downtown Coruscant. Unlike Jabba's stark, stone structure on Tatooine, Ziro the Hutt's castle was elaborately decorated inside and out.

Padmé was led into Ziro's throne room by two sentry droids. They were bulkier and more sinister-looking than regular battle droids, with glowing red eyes. The dark throne room was illuminated by lights on the ceiling that flashed in different colours. Ziro the Hutt sat on a round dais in the centre of the room. White spotlights around the dais lit up Ziro's huge, slug-like form. He was fatter than Jabba, if that was possible, and his yellow eyes were set more deeply in his wrinkled face.

Padmé was led to the dais. 'Your Majesty,' one of the droids announced, 'you have an important visitor.'

Padmé removed her hood. 'Greetings, Ziro. I am Senator Amidala of the Galactic Congress.'

'A Senator? In this neighbourhood?' Ziro asked,

in a very un-Hutt-like voice. Unlike his nephew, Ziro preferred to speak in the language of the Republic.

'I know that you are the uncle of Jabba the Hutt of Tatooine,' Padmé began. 'I have come to ask a favour of you. There has been a grave misunderstanding between Jabba and the Order of the Jedi.'

Ziro looked intrigued. 'How may I serve you, Senator?'

'I was hoping you and I could resolve this dispute and broker a treaty between the Republic and the great clan of the Hutts,' Padmé said.

This enraged the huge Hutt. 'A treaty! A treaty! A treaty is impossible. My nephew Jabba's son has been kidnapped by your Republic Jedi scum.'

'But, sir, there has been a misunderstanding,' Padmé tried to explain.

'There is no misunderstanding!' Ziro bellowed.

Now Padmé was angry. 'It is the Jedi who have *rescued* his son. If you can put me in touch with Jabba, I am confident I can convince him of the truth.'

'No! No more discussions!' Ziro said firmly. 'Escort her out!'

Ziro's stubbornness confounded Padmé. She decided to change tactics. 'Please, Ziro! Your nephew Jabba is in danger. You're being deceived!'

'I said, throw her out!' Ziro yelled.

A sentry droid stepped in front of Padmé, brandishing his weapon. He forcefully escorted her out of the throne room. The situation sank in as he pushed her into the turbolift. She had failed. As long as Jabba believed that Anakin had killed his son, Anakin's life was in danger.

That was not acceptable.

Padmé quickly swirled around, kicking the blaster out of the sentry droid's hands. She quickly sprinted through the doors of the turbolift as they were closing. The droid reached out and grabbed her cloak. She slipped out of it just as the doors closed. Then she marched back to the throne room. She was not leaving until Ziro agreed to help her contact Jabba, and she would not take no for an answer.

She approached the throne-room door and she flattened herself against a wall in the shadows. Ziro was talking to a hologram of Count Dooku. The Hutt looked flustered and nervous.

'Your plot is coming apart, Count Dooku! A Senator from the Republic was here! What if she finds out I helped you kidnap Jabba's son?'

'Don't worry,' Count Dooku said soothingly.

'I have convinced Jabba that the Jedi murdered his son and are on their way to kill him.'

'Jabba will slay the Jedi on sight!'

'Then the mighty Jedi Order will be forced to bring Jabba to justice, and you, my friend, will be left to take control of all the Hutt clans,' Count Dooku told him.

Ziro relaxed. 'Then my plot against my nephew Jabba has succeeded. But what about this meddling Senator?'

'If she continues with her investigation, have her meet with an accident with extreme prejudice,' Dooku suggested. 'I will have someone in the Senate cover it up for us.'

Padmé suddenly realized the danger she was in. She turned to run, but found herself face-to-face with two angry sentry droids.

She reached for the blaster on her belt and quickly fired at one of the droids. The other sentry droid grabbed her hand and squeezed tightly. She dropped the blaster, and the droid dragged her into the throne room, dropping her in front of Ziro.

'Count Dooku.' Padmé glared at the hologram. 'So, the poisonous traitor rears his ugly head once again.'

Dooku bowed politely. 'I'm equally delighted to make your acquaintance, Senator . . . Amidala, isn't it?'

Padmé stood up. 'I was just leaving.'

'I'm sorry, that cannot be permitted now,' Count Dooku said, his voice like ice. 'Ziro, this particular Senator is extremely valuable to my Separatist allies. They will pay a handsome price for her.'

Ziro's huge mouth smiled coldly. 'I like the sound of that! Take her to the dungeon!'

The sentry droid grabbed Padmé's arm and dragged her away. She struggled to break free.

'You will regret this, Ziro!' she cried.

'No, I think I will become rich with this!' the Hutt said, laughing. 'Thank you, Count Dooku. This has been a most profitable alliance.'

Count Dooku bowed. 'I will contact you when the Huttlet has been disposed of, your high exalted Master of the Hutts.'

CHAPTER TWENTY-ONE

Ahsoka opened the door of the *Twilight*. Holding Rotta in her arms, she stepped out of the damaged freighter on to the sandy surface of Tatooine. She looked out over the landscape, a barren stretch of nothingness broken up only by sand dunes scattered across the desert.

'Welcome home, Stinky,' she said.

Anakin came out of the ship behind them. He strapped on the backpack containing Rotta.

'Jabba's palace is on the far side of the Dune Sea,' he said. 'We'd better hurry if we're going to make it by morning.'

Rotta squealed, happy to be home. Ahsoka gazed out at the bleak horizon and frowned. Why couldn't they have crashed on the other side of the Dune Sea?

She stepped forward, and then heard a beep

behind her. Artoo stood on the ship's ramp, hesitant to follow.

'Oh, Artooie, it's just endless tracts of gritty, abrasive sand. I'll clean your servos later,' she promised. 'Come on.'

That was good enough for Artoo. He beeped and rolled down the ramp after her.

The planet's twin suns were slowly sinking behind them as they trudged across the landscape. Ahsoka struggled to keep up with Anakin's long strides. It was going to be a long journey, and Anakin had been silent since they had arrived on Tatooine. Ahsoka wondered what had happened in his past that could upset him this much.

She decided to try to reach out. She hurried ahead until she was walking by his side.

'Master Yoda has a saying, "Old sins cast long shadows." Do you know what he means by that?' Ahsoka asked.

'He means your past can ruin your future if you allow it,' Anakin replied. 'But you forget that it was Master Skywalker who said, "I don't want to talk about my past."'

'Okay, fine,' Ahsoka said. 'There is so much more we can talk about out here. Like the desert.'

'The desert is merciless,' Anakin said matter-of-factly. 'It takes everything from you.'

Ahsoka looked up at him sympathetically. *It takes everything from you.* Whatever had happened to Anakin on Tatooine, it must have been awful.

'That's a happy thought,' she said, trying to sound cheerful. 'It won't take *us*, Master. Right, Artooie?'

Beep!

They walked on and on in silence. Ahsoka searched her mind for a topic of conversation that wouldn't lead to bad memories for Anakin. Master Yoda's favourite colour, maybe? No, that wouldn't do. She sighed. At least this part of their journey wasn't dangerous, but it sure was boring.

Then Anakin abruptly stopped in front of her, sensing something. Ahsoka noticed something, too.

'We're not alone,' she said. She could feel the strange ripple in the Force. It made her uneasy.

'I sense it, too,' Anakin said. 'It's the dark side of the Force.'

Rotta let out a frightened squeak and pulled the flap of the backpack over his head.

'Whatever it is, it's coming for Rotta,' Anakin said. 'Time to split up.'

'We'll face it together, Master,' Ahsoka said bravely.

'Not this time, Snips,' Anakin said. 'I have a far more important mission for you.'

'More important than keeping you alive?' Ahsoka asked.

'Ahsoka, I need you to trust me on this one,' Anakin said firmly. 'Now, here's the plan . . .'

CHAPTER TWENTY-TWO

The sentry droid confiscated Padmé's blaster and hologram projector and threw them on to the ground. It shoved Padmé into a cell and the barred door hissed shut. The droid faced the cell door with its own blaster poised to fire. Four battle droids lined the walls outside the cell, prepared to back up the sentry. Padmé glared at them defiantly from behind the bars.

Next to the sentry droid, her holoprojector began to flash and buzz. Someone was trying to contact Padmé. A flash of hope surged through her.

'What's that?' one of the battle droids asked. The slow-witted droid had never seen a holoprojector before.

'Don't touch that!' Padmé warned. 'Whatever you do, keep away from that. Please, I beg you!'

One of the droids took her bait. 'Could be dangerous. I'd better check it out.' He reached down and picked up the holoprojector, activating it.

A holographic image of C-3PO appeared. Padmé's bronze protocol droid shook his head nervously.

'At last you answered! Oh, I've been so worried,' Threepio cried. Then he noticed the battle droid staring curiously at him. 'Wait, who are you? You're not Mistress Padmé.'

'Threepio, get help!' Padmé called from her cell. 'I'm being held by Ziro the Hutt!'

'You're in trouble! I knew it!' Threepio cried. 'Wait, wait . . . oh!'

The sentry droid knocked the holoprojector out of the battle droid's hand and then crushed it with his heavy foot. Padmé stepped back from the bars of the cell.

She wasn't sure if Threepio had heard the message, but she had to stay hopeful. She had a feeling she didn't have much time left.

Over on Tatooine, Anakin walked through the desert by himself, Rotta's pack on his back. He looked up to see a hooded figure approaching, riding a speeder bike. It was Count Dooku. He stopped the bike, dismounted and walked towards Anakin, his cloak flapping in the wind. Anakin ignited his lightsaber and held it defensively in front of him.

'Surrender the Huttlet or die, Skywalker,' Dooku commanded. He extended his right hand, and jagged streaks of Sith lightning blasted from his fingertips, lighting up the dark desert. Anakin held out his lightsaber to absorb the energy.

Dooku reached for his own lightsaber next and swung the weapon at Anakin, forcing him back.

'Your training has come a long way, boy,' Dooku said.

Anakin thrust his lightsaber forward, lunging at the Sith Lord. Dooku knocked back the blow with his lightsaber blade.

'Ah, now I remember,' Dooku said. 'This was your home planet, wasn't it? I sense your strong feelings. Feelings of pain. Loss.'

Dooku was trying to bait him, Anakin knew. He had to stay focused. He whipped up his hand, commanding a tornado of sand to rise from the dunes. It swirled around Dooku, knocking him off his feet.

Dooku jumped up and hurled the whirling sand back at Anakin. The Jedi fell, losing his lightsaber.

Dooku charged at him, swinging his blade. Anakin recovered his lightsaber just in time, parrying the attack in one swift movement. Dooku slashed out again, slicing Anakin's backpack in half. He grinned triumphantly.

'You've failed, Jedi,' he gloated. 'I have just killed Jabba's son.'

'You've fallen for my little trick, Count,' Anakin replied. He tossed off the backpack and a hail of chopped-up rocks spilled out on the sand.

'It's nothing but rocks,' he said. 'The Huttlet is with my Padawan, safely at Jabba's palace.'

Count Dooku was not shaken. 'I expected such treachery from a Jedi. I assure you my web is strong enough to catch your insignificant little Padawan.'

'She's more powerful than you think,' Anakin shot back.

'You deceive yourself!' Count Dooku yelled. He charged at Anakin again.

On the other side of the Dune Sea, Ahsoka climbed over a sand dune. The two suns were rising over Jabba's palace. Rotta gurgled happily on her back, and Artoo followed behind. Ahsoka smiled. She was almost there!

Then a warning flashed through her brain. *Danger!* She quickly ignited her lightsaber.

Three MagnaGuards erupted from out of the sand, blocking her path to the palace. The three droids activated their attack staffs, which began to crackle with deadly energy.

Then they charged at Ahsoka.

CHAPTER TWENTY-THREE

Anakin and Count Dooku exchanged blows, their glowing lightsabers streaking the dark desert sky as they fought. Dooku abruptly stopped and took out a holoprojector from his cloak.

'Look, I have a message from your Padawan,' he sneered.

Anakin hacked at Dooku's hand, knocking the holoprojector into the sand. A blue hologram image projected on to the dunes, showing the three MagnaGuards fighting Ahsoka. Then the hologram flickered out.

'After my droids kill Jabba's son, they will deliver your Padawan to him for punishment,' Dooku said, cackling at his own cleverness. 'I can't imagine that he will be merciful.'

Anakin jumped to the top of a dune, looming

over Count Dooku. He had the upper hand now, but chose not to use it.

Instead, he somersaulted off the dune, landing on Dooku's speeder. He raced off into the desert. There was no time to take down Dooku now.

I'm coming, Ahsoka!

Ziro the Hutt sat on his throne, his yellow eyes glittering with anger. Two sentry droids brought Padmé before him, flanked by the four battle droids from the dungeon.

'You tried to call for help, Senator,' Ziro said. 'I believe you are too dangerous to be kept alive!'

The sentry droids pointed their blasters at Padmé.

'Killing a Galactic Senator, here on Coruscant,' Padmé said, her voice strong. 'Are you out of your mind?'

'I have powerful friends in the Senate. I'm not afraid of –'

Boom! An explosion rocked the building.

'What is that?' Ziro bellowed, just as Republic shock troopers stormed into the throne room.

'Run for it!' Ziro yelled. He began to slither off his dais.

The shock troopers opened fire on the droids.

Padmé knocked the blaster out of the hands of the sentry droid next to her and ran up next to Ziro.

'Stop, Ziro! Stop right where you are!'

Threepio appeared in the doorway, spotted Padmé and hurried over to her.

'Mistress Padmé! Are you all right? Was I too late?'

'Threepio!' Padmé felt like cheering. 'Your timing was perfect.'

'Oh, thank the maker!' the droid said. 'I am so relieved.'

Commander Fox, the leader of the shock troopers, ran to Padmé's side.

'Should we arrest the Hutt, Senator?'

The heavily armed clone troopers surrounded the Hutt. He frantically waved his arms as he struggled to explain himself.

'I had no choice! Dooku said he'd kill me if I didn't help him kidnap Jabba's son. You have to believe me. I love that Huttlet!'

Padmé grinned. She had the Hutt right where she wanted him. 'Oh, I believe you.'

The MagnaGuards attacked Ahsoka, staffs blazing. She used her lightsaber to deflect the blows, but she was outnumbered. She jumped back, landing on top of a small sand dune.

Artoo rolled forward, extending his buzz saw. It wasn't much of a weapon, but it was all he had. A MagnaGuard clubbed him, knocking him down.

'Artoo!' Ahsoka yelled. She took a deep breath. 'Three against two . . . Stinky, you watch my back.'

One of the MagnaGuards charged up the dune, slashing at her with his staff. She dodged it but felt the sizzling electricity graze her arm. She thrust back at the guard with her lightsaber, making contact. The guard tumbled backwards.

Ahsoka leaped to the next dune. She might not be able to battle them, but maybe she could outrun them and get to the castle.

A MagnaGuard raced towards her and aimed a blow at Rotta's head. Ahsoka blocked the attack, but took a blow to her arm from another MagnaGuard. She tumbled down the dune.

Rotta squealed, coughing up a mouthful of sand.

'I thought you liked to play in the sand,' Ahsoka joked, but the Huttlet was not happy. Ahsoka jumped to her feet.

She could see that the MagnaGuards had almost reached the top of the dune above her. Thinking quickly, she circled around the bottom of the dune. Then she climbed back up on the other side and looked down.

The confused guards stood at the bottom of the dune, wondering where Ahsoka was. Perfect. She jumped down from the dune, slicing one of the guards in half as she landed.

Two more to go!

Then the sound of a whirrring engine filled the air. Ahsoka looked into the sky to see a speeder bike racing past her. She could tell that it was Anakin piloting it, but he didn't see her or the MagnaGuards.

'Master! Master! Over here!' she yelled. But Anakin kept riding towards the castle. Ahsoka sighed. 'He never listens.'

Ahsoka quickly turned back to the remaining MagnaGuards.

'All right, Stick-Tinnies, you are going back to Dooku in pieces!' she informed them.

While Ahsoka battled the MagnaGuards, Anakin pulled up in front of Jabba's castle. He raced inside the door. Several palace guards pointed their weapons at him. They were Nikto, from planet Kintan. Their long, leathery faces stared angrily at Anakin.

TC-70 appeared between them.

'Where is my Padawan?' Anakin asked.

'This way,' the droid said. 'Your weapon, please.'

Anakin reluctantly handed over his lightsaber. The guards descended on him, herding him into the castle. In the throne room, Jabba lay on his dais. A nervous hush fell over the room as Anakin entered.

'This is Jedi Knight Anakin Skywalker,' TC-70 said. 'As Count Dooku said, your son is not with him.'

'What? Your son's not here?' Anakin said, worried. That meant Ahsoka was not here, either.

The Nikto pushed Anakin in front of Jabba.

'JEDI POODOO!'

'Where's Ahsoka?' Anakin asked.

Jabba glowered down at him. 'NOBATA BARGON! EECHUTA ROTTA ME PEEDUNKEE MUFKIN WAJEEKEE!'

Anakin extended his hand and his lightsaber flew from TC-70's hands into his. He ignited it and extended the blue blade to Jabba's throat.

'What have you done with my Padawan?' he asked, his voice rising with anger.

'AHH! SKYWALKER KILLYE!' Jabba cried.

'You came here to kill Jabba,' TC-70 accused.

'Mighty Jabba, I came here to negotiate,' Anakin said, but he did not lower his blade.

'AAAGH! OOCHUTA MAKA MEDI WAH!' Jabba raged.

'You came here to die,' the protocol droid calmly translated.

The Nikto guards surrounded Anakin, weapons drawn. He tensed. He probably couldn't fight all of them . . . but he would try.

'Stop!'

Ahsoka's voice filled the throne room. She marched in, carrying Rotta. She was exhausted and panting; her skin was scratched and dirty. But the MagnaGuard fighters she'd left out in the desert were in a lot worse shape.

Anakin lowered his lightsaber. 'Most patient Jabba, your son has arrived. Alive and well.'

Jabba narrowed his eyes suspiciously; he couldn't see Ahsoka through the guards. He grunted and nodded for them to let her pass. She marched through them.

'He is alive, isn't he?' Anakin whispered to her.

'And still stinky,' Ahsoka assured him.

Anakin flashed her a proud smile. She lifted up the flap of the backpack to reveal Rotta's sleeping face. Jabba looked down, not sure if his son was alive.

'ROTTA, ME PEEDUNKEE?'

Rotta's eyes popped open. He gurgled happily, and then gave a loud burp.

'PEEDUNKEE MUFKIN!' Jabba cried. He looked at the boy with relief and then looked up at the Jedi angrily.

'NOBATA! KEELYA JEDI!' he bellowed.

'You are to be executed immediately,' TC-70 informed them.

Ahsoka and Anakin looked at each other in shock.

'What?' they cried in unison.

CHAPTER TWENTY-FOUR

Ahsoka and Anakin ignited their lightsabers. The Nikto guards moved in closer, ready to fire.

'Does this always happen to you?' Ahsoka asked.

'Everywhere I go,' Anakin replied.

Rotta started to cry. On the dais, Jabba's holoprojector began to beep.

'Your uncle Ziro is contacting us,' TC-70 announced.

But the hologram that appeared wasn't Ziro, it was Padmé. Seeing her image stirred Anakin's heart.

'Greetings, honourable Jabba,' Padmé said. 'I am Senator Amidala of the Galactic Senate. I have discovered a plot against you by one of your own.'

A hologram of Ziro the Hutt materialized near Padmé. Jabba grunted at the sight of his uncle.

'Your uncle will admit that he conspired with Count Dooku to kidnap your son and frame the Jedi for the crime,' Padmé said.

Jabba reared up on his huge belly, furious. 'ZIRO! TAHJAH WOOCHEESKA!'

'OONEETA MABONGA JABBA!' Ziro replied, denying the accusation.

'ROTTA KO WEEWAH!'

'NOBATA JABBA! IT WAS COUNT DOOKU!' Ziro pleaded.

Jabba had heard enough. He motioned for Ziro to get out of his sight. The contrite Hutt crawled out of the hologram.

'WAHH! JANAGA ZIRO KEEZ!' Jabba announced.

TC-70 translated. 'Ziro will be dealt with by the Hutt family . . . most severely.'

'Perhaps you will allow the Republic to use your trade routes and hostilities can come to an end,' Padmé suggested.

Jabba considered the offer. Then he looked at Ahsoka and Anakin and laughed.

'HA! HA! HA! KOOTU BARGON TAGWA!'

'Jabba agrees,' the protocol droid said. 'A treaty is in order.'

'You will not regret this, Jabba,' Padmé promised.

Ahsoka and Anakin smiled at each other, relieved. Their mission was a success!

Jabba nodded. 'KLOON WEETU REPUBLICA HUTT MOOKEE!'

'The clone armies may move through Jabba's territories,' TC-70 informed them.

The Nikto guards lowered their blasters. Anakin and Ahsoka turned off their lightsabers. Rotta gave a happy squeal.

Anakin looked up at Padmé's image.

'Senator. You have my undying . . . gratitude,' he told her.

Padmé smiled warmly back at him.

'No, Master Skywalker. It is I, and the Republic, who owe you thanks,' she replied.

The two stared at each other for a moment . . . perhaps a moment too long. Ahsoka noticed the exchange.

Another of Master's mysteries, she mused.

The hologram faded from view. Anakin and Ahsoka bowed respectfully to Jabba.

'Jabba would be most appreciative if you bring Dooku to justice for his crimes against the Hutts,' the protocol droid told them.

'You can count on it, Jabba,' Anakin said, grinning.

Count Dooku rocketed away from Tatooine in his spacecraft. He had bad news to deliver, and he wasn't looking forward to it.

But there was no point in putting it off. He activated his holoprojector and transmitted a message to his Master, Darth Sidious.

'It is unfortunate, Master,' Dooku said. 'The Jedi Armies will now have their supply routes to the Outer Rim. Our fight has become far more difficult.'

Darth Sidious hid in the folds of his black hooded cloak. He answered Dooku in a slithering voice. 'Allow the Jedi their small victory, my friend, for the engines of this war turn in our favour.'

Back on Tatooine, Ahsoka and Anakin stood outside Jabba's palace. A Republic gunship landed in the sand. Obi-Wan and Yoda exited from the ramp. Obi-Wan gave the Jedi an approving glance.

Ahsoka beamed up at Anakin, and he smiled down at her. A wave of pride and confidence surged through her.

When she first went to study at the Jedi Temple years ago, she had dreamed of someday becoming a Jedi Knight. That day had seemed far, far away.

Now, it seemed closer than ever.